"I take it you're

Caroline gave him
think that?"

Sitting on her couch, Mike ~~~ ~~~~~~ ~~~ ~~ble for his own good. And too sexy for *her* good.

"Well, either there's no one or your father doesn't like him. Otherwise he wouldn't be matchmaking."

She jerked her head from his shoulder. "My personal life is none of your business, Sheriff."

"If your father is going to matchmake, it seems to involve me, too," he shot back.

Caroline turned away. "I'm sorry. I'll tell him no. I mean, I'll tell him you won't do."

"But I think I would do." Mike pulled her gently back against him and lifted her chin. "You know, I've been wanting to kiss you all night." Then he lowered his head and did.

When their lips met, his power over her was obvious. Incredible. Overwhelming. His kiss was everything she'd hoped for. And couldn't have. She put her hands on his chest and pushed. "Mike, we—we need to stop. I'm not going to get married."

He smiled, dark and mischievous. "I don't remember proposing," he whispered. Then he leaned in to trail hot kisses down her neck. "But a little loving might persuade me."

Dear Friends,

I know from your e-mails that you've been eager for more Randall books, so I'm glad to deliver another Randall story to you. Caroline has been waiting for her story for some time. I hope you enjoy it. And I do plan to continue writing more Randall books in the future, but I am now starting a new series for Harlequin American Romance, which I am very excited about.

Once I got started with the new series, I found myself creating a brand-new family. I think everyone knows now that family is an important theme for me. In THE CHILDREN OF TEXAS, I'm introducing a family to itself. The six Barlow siblings found themselves separated from one another when their parents were killed. Four of the children were adopted. The two older children went through the foster care system.

It is the youngest Barlow, Vanessa, whose adoptive mother sets in motion the search for her daughter's siblings. Some of the results are unexpected, but bringing a family together after more than twenty years is not an easy task.

The series begins in January 2004 with the novella "Family Unveiled," available in the Harlequin anthology *Private Scandals*, and will continue in 2004 in the Harlequin American Romance line. I hope you'll enjoy this family as much as you've told me you enjoy the Randalls.

Happy reading,

Judy Christenberry

Judy Christenberry

A RANDALL RETURNS

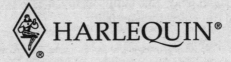

HARLEQUIN®

TORONTO • NEW YORK • LONDON
AMSTERDAM • PARIS • SYDNEY • HAMBURG
STOCKHOLM • ATHENS • TOKYO • MILAN • MADRID
PRAGUE • WARSAW • BUDAPEST • AUCKLAND

ISBN 0-373-75004-8

A RANDALL RETURNS

Copyright © 2003 by Judy Christenberry.

This edition published by arrangement with Harlequin Books S.A.

® and TM are trademarks of the publisher. Trademarks indicated with ® are registered in the United States Patent and Trademark Office, the Canadian Trade Marks Office and in other countries.

Visit us at www.eHarlequin.com

Printed in U.S.A.

ABOUT THE AUTHOR

Judy Christenberry has been writing romances for fifteen years because she loves happy endings as much as her readers do. A former French teacher, Judy now devotes herself to writing full-time. She hopes readers have as much fun reading her stories as she does writing them. She spends her spare time reading, watching her favorite sports teams and keeping track of her two daughters. Judy resides in Texas.

Books by Judy Christenberry

HARLEQUIN AMERICAN ROMANCE

HARLEQUIN INTRIGUE

*Brides for Brothers
†Tots for Texans

THE RANDALLS

THE RANDALL BROTHERS

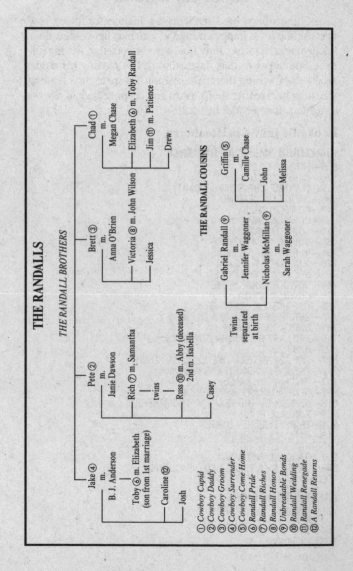

Jake ④
m.
B. J. Anderson
— Toby ⑥ m. Elizabeth
(son from 1st marriage)
— Caroline ⑫
— Josh

Pete ②
m.
Janie Dawson
— Rich ⑦ m. Samantha
— twins
— Russ ⑩ m. Abby (deceased)
2nd m. Isabella
— Casey

Brett ③
m.
Anna O'Brien
— Victoria ⑧ m. John Wilson
— Jessica

Chad ①
m.
Megan Chase
— Elizabeth ⑥ m. Toby Randall
— Jim ⑪ m. Patience
— Drew

THE RANDALL COUSINS

Gabriel Randall ⑨
m.
Jennifer Waggoner
— John

Nicholas McMillan ⑨
m.
Sarah Waggoner
— Melissa

Griffin ⑤
m.
Camille Chase

Twins
separated
at birth

① *Cowboy Cupid*
② *Cowboy Daddy*
③ *Cowboy Groom*
④ *Cowboy Surrender*
⑤ *Cowboy Come Home*
⑥ *Randall Pride*
⑦ *Randall Riches*
⑧ *Randall Honor*
⑨ *Unbreakable Bonds*
⑩ *Randall Wedding*
⑪ *Randall Renegade*
⑫ *A Randall Returns*

Chapter One

Mike Davis stood outside the Sheriff's Office on Main Street in Rawhide. The cold, frosty morning was quite different from those he'd known back in Chicago. Not the temperature, but the clean air, the lack of traffic, the friendly waves from passersby. Yes, he thought, Rawhide, Wyoming, was light-years away from the big city.

A few weeks ago he'd made a momentous change in his life when his uncle had called him. Bill Metzger had been Rawhide's sheriff for two decades, until sidelined by a sudden heart attack. Though he'd survived, it kick-started his retirement, and he was moving to Arizona, looking for lots of warmth and no stress.

But he wanted to leave the town of Rawhide safe. So he'd called Mike. A former army M.P. and then a Chicago policeman, Mike was Bill's choice of successor based on ability, not nepotism. Uncle Bill—actually he was Mike's second cousin—had told him he had a year before the next election. By then, the citizenry would love him and he'd be a shoo-in to win the position.

Mike drew another deep, icy breath and looked around the town he'd sworn to protect. Compared to Chicago, this little town in the middle of Wyoming was downright peaceful. He walked down Main Street, looking at the two-story structures, many with wooden porches, and greeted the townsfolk who ventured out this early on a December morning.

He noticed an SUV parked at a snug house on the next street. It had Illinois plates.

That house had been pointed out to him specifically. Jake Randall, one of Bill's old friends, had asked Mike to keep an eye on it. He'd bought the place for his daughter, who was due home soon.

Though Jake hadn't said where she was living, Mike assumed she was coming home from college— probably from the University of Wyoming in Laramie. Most of the local kids went there. Besides, Mike couldn't imagine anyone from Wyoming moving to Illinois. And he wouldn't expect some college girl to drive a big SUV.

With a frown, he stepped off the wooden porch of the sandwich shop and crossed to the back street. He found the door of the house ajar. Drawing his gun, he stepped quietly into the living room. He couldn't help but notice the house was fully furnished and very attractive. If he hadn't known the Randalls had money, he'd know it now.

A sound from the next room had him stepping quietly behind the open door. A slim woman with long dark hair and beautiful skin came into view. This was no college coed, Mike thought. In fact, she looked to be around thirty. Not Jake's daughter, obviously, so why was she in Randall's house?

"Stop right there and put your hands up!" He waited for her to comply, but she didn't. Glaring at him, she walked forward calmly and confidently.

"Who are you?"

"Sheriff Davis. Who are you?"

"Where is Sheriff Metzger?"

"Lady, I'm arresting you for breaking and entering. Put your hands behind your back." Again he waited for her to do as he asked.

"You've got to be kidding!"

"Do you have any ID?"

"No, I don't. Want to frisk me?"

Her flippant response irritated Mike. He took his work seriously, and she was thumbing her nose at him.

He grabbed her arm and whirled her around. Before she knew what was happening, he had her in cuffs. Then, as she'd suggested, he briskly frisked her.

"Don't touch me!" she shouted.

"Lady, I have to do my job. Let's take a little walk to the jail. You can make your one phone call there."

She gave him an icy stare. "Oh, yeah. I can't wait."

Mike normally would have questioned her first, but her attitude annoyed him. If she wanted to play hard-ball, disrespect his badge, she'd have to pay the price.

At the office, only one deputy was in yet. Mike waved at him and took the angry young woman to his office. "Give me the number and I'll dial it for you."

She lifted her chin. "For your sake, I'll call Jon Wilson, but I don't know his number."

Mike frowned. "For my sake?"

"Yes. Do you know the number?"

"Yeah, I do." He dialed it and asked for Dr. Wilson. "Jon? It's Mike Davis. I arrested a woman in that house Jake Randall owns. She wanted me to call you for her one phone call.

"Here she is," he said, after Jon agreed to speak to her.

"Hi, Jon," the woman said softly. "I'm here."

After a moment, she stepped away from the phone. "He's coming right over."

Mike frowned again. "Why would he do that?"

She gave him a superior smile. "You can ask him when he gets here."

"Fine. Can I trust you to sit quietly until he comes, or do I need to put you in a cell?"

"Suit yourself." Instead of waiting for him to make a decision, she sank down in the chair beside his desk like a model, showing off her slim legs below a suede skirt.

Mike had a niggling feeling he'd been set up.

The door to the office flew open and Tori Wilson, a Randall and now Jon's wife, screamed, "Caroline!" She hugged the woman in handcuffs. "What happened?"

"You'll have to ask this Mickey Mouse sheriff. What happened to Sheriff Metzger?"

Mike stiffened, gritting his teeth. To respond to her taunts would do no good.

"Caroline! Why are you acting like this? Sheriff Metzger retired because of a heart attack. This is his cousin, Sheriff Davis."

Anger colored Caroline's face. "Why do you think I'm acting like this? I'm in cuffs!"

"Didn't you tell him who you are?" Jon asked from the doorway.

"I didn't see the need." She turned and stared at Mike again.

"Sheriff, I'll clear this up. There's no need—" Jon began, but a noise outside the office stopped him. "Uh-oh."

"What's wrong?" Mike asked, taking a step forward.

When he saw the big man who entered into the office, he didn't need Jon's answer. Jake Randall. From the look on Jake's face as he took in the scene and turned hard eyes on him, Mike knew the woman in cuffs was none other than Jake's beloved daughter, who was going to live in that house. Mike figured his career as sheriff of Rawhide was going to be short-lived.

"Caroline!" Jake exclaimed, rushing to embrace the young woman. Then he turned to Mike. "Why is she in handcuffs?"

"I'm sorry, Mr. Randall. I didn't know she was your daughter. I saw an out-of-state SUV outside the house, and the door open. I caught her inside."

"Didn't she identify herself?"

"No, sir. I asked for ID. She didn't provide any. Nor did she give me her name." Mike drew a deep breath and reached for the key to release the cuffs.

Before he could do so, however, Jake stopped him. "She gave you lip, didn't she?"

Mike gave a small smile. "None that I haven't heard before. I apologize for—"

"You have nothing to apologize for." He turned

to his daughter. "Caroline, you know better than to act like this. You're the one who should apologize."

Mike stared at the man. Someone who stood up for the law instead of his own child? That was rare.

"Okay, so I should've told him, but he upset me. He acted as if I was a criminal. Sheriff Metzger would never have—"

"No, he wouldn't have, because he knew you. All you had to do was identify yourself to Sheriff Davis. Instead, you caused all this commotion. I'm ashamed of you, young lady."

She turned and, much to Mike's surprise, apologized. "I'm sorry, Sheriff Davis. I was in a bad mood and I took it out on you."

"I think you should keep her locked up for twenty-four hours," Jake told Mike.

"Dad!" Caroline Randall said, obviously startled by her father's response. "You wouldn't—"

"*I* wouldn't keep you overnight, Miss Randall. Our jail is not for childish pranksters." Mike turned her around and unlocked the cuffs. Then he indicated the door with a nod of his head.

"My apologies, Sheriff," she said again. "And by the way, it's *Dr.* Randall. I'll be partnering with Jon at the clinic."

Her words were polite, but she clearly hadn't forgiven him for not bowing down and bringing flowers.

"I'm sure you'll be very welcome, Dr. Randall." Mike turned and extended his hand to Jake. "I apologize for misunderstanding the situation."

"It wasn't your fault. Don't think any more about it," Jake exclaimed.

"Yes, sir." Mike breathed a sigh of relief. He'd

already fallen in love with Rawhide. The thought of going back to Chicago gave him a headache.

CAROLINE WANTED TO CRY as she got into her father's truck. She'd disappointed him. "I really am sorry, Dad."

"I don't understand why you acted that way. We taught you to respect the law. What happened?" He looked at her. "Was it living in the big city?"

"No, Dad," she said with a sigh. "It's just... transitions are hard."

After a moment of silence, Jake, with a heavy heart, said, "You didn't want to come home." It wasn't a question.

Caroline sniffed back tears. "Not exactly. I want to see everyone, but...I'm alone. I don't have a family. I won't have a lot of time. And I—I don't know how I'll fit in!"

"What are you talking about, honey? You've got family all over the place!"

"No family of my own, I mean."

"Who do you think your mother and I are?" Jake roared, clearly getting upset.

The last thing she needed was to have her father angry at her. "Oh, Dad, you know what I mean."

"No, I don't!"

She didn't explain. She couldn't. She adored her father, so much so that she never wanted to disappoint him. So she hid the truth. And that was why she should've stayed in Chicago.

"Well?"

"I can't explain, Dad. I'll—I'll talk to Mom!"

"Why her and not me?" He sounded hurt, which made her feel doubly guilty.

"She's a woman. It's hard to explain to a man."

Jake didn't look happy, but he said nothing.

"Where is Mom, by the way? She didn't want to come with you?"

"She's on a call out at the Johnson ranch. Sick cattle, I hear. She only works part-time now, but she traded days to be here tomorrow when you were supposed to arrive. Red was baking a chocolate cake, and Mildred was making a big chicken spaghetti casserole. You know, the kind you love."

"Oh, dear. I've ruined everything, haven't I?"

He didn't spare her. "Pretty much." Then he added, "By the way, your mom and all your aunts worked hard to make the house nice. If you don't like it, lie."

"Oh no, Dad. I love it. It's…it's wonderful, especially the office."

"Good. They only had a couple of months, you know. As soon as they finished the wedding, they started in on the house."

"How are Jim and Patience?" She remembered how happy her uncle Chad's son Jim had sounded when he'd told her about Patience. Though glad for him, she couldn't help but feel sorry that she hadn't found someone herself. And never would.

"Good," her dad replied. "They're living in Red and Mildred's old house."

"That's what Mom said."

"How long you been feeling this way?"

At his abrupt change of topic Caroline gave her

father a sharp look before averting her eyes. "What way?"

"Like you didn't want to come home. I'm figuring four years. Am I right?"

With a sigh, she said, "Yes, Dad. Four years."

"Right after that accident you were in?"

She nodded.

Her father didn't say anything else as he drove the truck up to the house. She sat up straight, cleared her throat and said, "I'll be sure to apologize to everyone for surprising them a day early."

Again he didn't reply.

With relief, Caroline recognized her mother's vehicle. "Mom's back!"

Within seconds, B.J. Randall came bounding out of the house. She was in such a hurry she didn't even put on a coat.

Caroline threw herself from the truck into her mother's arms. Tears flowed as they held each other close. When B.J. finally released her, Jake put his arm around his wife.

"You're not wearing a coat, honey. Come on in the house before you get sick."

B.J. laughed at him but she willingly turned toward the house, one arm around her husband's waist and the other around Caroline.

Inside, Red and Mildred hugged her, as did her younger brother, Josh, and her half brother, Toby, who held his toddler daughter. Caroline raved to the aunts about her new house, letting them all know she appreciated their efforts. Noticing her new cousin-in-law, Patience, standing off to the side, she greeted her, too. She'd known Jim's wife, Patience, before but they hadn't been good friends because Patience was much younger.

But Caroline did remember her sister, Faith, and expressed sorrow about Patience's loss. And she welcomed her to the family.

"Okay, okay, you've greeted everyone. Now come upstairs with me," her mother insisted.

Caroline readily agreed, but she felt her father's gaze on her. She faced him and nodded slightly. Yes, she would tell her mom why she'd been reluctant to come home. And her mother would tell Jake. They never kept secrets from each other.

Caroline followed her upstairs to her parents' sitting room. "Oh, Mom, you look good. How's everything?"

"Everything's fine, dear, especially since you've come home."

Caroline sighed. "Dad's already talked to you, hasn't he?"

Her mother nodded. "While you were greeting everyone else. He said you wouldn't tell him why you didn't want to come home. Are we too...provincial, too much in the sticks, for you?"

"Never, Mom. I love all of you, I love the ranch and I love Rawhide."

"Then why have you refused to come home for the past four years?" She steadily gazed at her daughter, waiting.

Caroline shrugged. "My schedule was so hectic and—"

She stopped because her mother was shaking her head.

"The truth, please, Caro."

Caroline sighed. "You always could tell if I tried to slip one by you," she said with a small smile. "The problem has nothing to do with the family, or with Rawhide. Well, not really. It's me, Mom." Tears welled in her eyes, but she fought them.

"Darling, what are you talking about? There's nothing wrong with you!"

"Yes, there is." Caroline bowed her head, gathering strength for what she had to say. "Mom, when I was in that wreck, I sustained permanent injury." Gooseflesh rose on her skin merely from thinking about the crash that had demolished her car and put her in the hospital for a week. A couple had run a red light and blindsided her. It had happened so fast she hadn't known what had hit her, until she was told in the hospital.

"What are you talking about?"

"Scar tissue built up and the doctor said it would be almost impossible for me to get pregnant."

Her mother took her in her arms. "Sweetheart, I'm sorry. But that's no reason to not come home."

"Isn't it, Mom? Rawhide, headquarters of the happy Randalls, where matchmaking is rampant, followed immediately by lots of babies." She drew a deep breath. "Except for poor Caroline. She's barren, poor thing."

Her mother said nothing. Caroline continued, "In Chicago, I stayed busy. No one thought it strange that a pediatrician didn't have an armful of babies. I had my career and I was damn good at it. But here…here it's different. I don't want people to pity me!"

B.J. held her close. "I don't want you to leave. I love you so much. But because I love you, I'll understand if you want to go back to Chicago. Your father and I will come see you there."

Caroline pulled away from her mother. "Dad won't feel that way. I've disappointed him."

"Caro, your father loves you more than anything in the world. No, he won't want you to go. But like me, he'll tell you to go rather than see you miserable."

"It's too late now. I left my job and my—well, Don is with someone else now."

"He is? But I thought you two—"

"Would marry and live happily ever after?" Caroline gave a bitter laugh. "No. It seems he had a nurse on the side. When she turned up pregnant, he married her."

"Oh, dear." B.J. Randall held her only daughter close. "A mother always dreams of a wonderful future for her children. But, Caroline, you've *got* a wonderful future. There's more to life than having babies. You're a doctor now, able to save lives. If you want children, there are plenty who have no mother. You don't have to bear them yourself."

Caroline wiped the tears away. Her mother was telling her what she'd told herself millions of times. But coming home reopened the wounds, made the pain fresh again.

"Thanks, Mom. But—but it's so hard here."

"I know. That's why your father and I won't oppose your returning to Chicago."

Caroline tried to stop her tears. "Return to what? I don't belong there, either. I might as well be here, with the ones I love."

"Did you and Don use—I mean, I assume you and he—"

"Slept together? Yes, Mom, we did. I'm thirty years old, you know, not some sheltered virgin. And no, we didn't use birth control. And nothing happened, Mom. I never got pregnant."

"I'm sorry. I didn't mean to pry. Have you been to a fertility specialist?"

"No. I read my charts, though. And I know the prognosis."

"I meant what I said. We don't love you because you're a possible producer of grandchildren. We love you because of you. I only asked those questions because I want you to be happy."

"I know, Mom." Caroline pressed her lips tightly together. "I'm okay. I—I dreaded telling you about it. And because I was upset, I took revenge on the new sheriff. I apologized, of course, but I embarrassed Dad, too. I'm so sorry."

Her mom hugged her again. "I'm just glad you're home. Now tell me the truth," she said with a forced smile. "Do you really like the house?"

"I love it. The living room is comfortable and bright, and my office is wonderful! And it's all done in classic decor. No frills. You remembered." She gave her mother a shaky smile.

"How could I forget? I did your bedroom in pink ruffles, and there you were—five years old and screaming because you wanted a tailored blue."

"I guess I wasn't an easy child," Caroline said softly.

"I didn't want a doll to dress up, sweetheart. I had the best gift of all, a strong, determined person who knew what she wanted. You've never disappointed me.''

''Oh, Mom!'' Caroline buried her face on her mother's shoulder and finally released all those tears she'd been holding back.

WHEN B.J. EXPLAINED their daughter's behavior, Jake turned away from his wife. ''We should've sued those people who crashed into her! Had them arrested!'' His voice was angry. ''We let them get off scot-free!''

''That wouldn't have helped Caroline then or now, Jake. And she didn't want to sue.''

''I know, B.J., but it's my job to protect her, and I didn't!'' he raged, shame mixing with his anger.

B.J. put her arms around her beloved husband. ''Jake, you do everything humanly possible to protect your family. Caroline knows that you'll always be there for her.''

''I suggested she be thrown in jail today. She may never forgive me!''

''Honey, she knows she was at fault.''

''Yeah, but I should've—''

B.J. covered his lips with her hand. ''Honey, there's nothing we can do, except love her. I told her if she wanted to go back to Chicago, we'd be all right with that.''

''No! I can't— Is she going to go?''

''No. That doctor she was seeing—Don—was two-timing her with a nurse who got pregnant.''

Jake looked even more outraged. ''I'll kill him!''

B.J. held on to him, expecting his reaction. Her husband was a man of action. When he had a target, he'd take aim.

"Jake, there's nothing you can do. Even if you could convince the man to come back to Caroline, would you want her married to a jerk like that?"

"No. But I could redecorate his face so he might remember his stupid mistake!"

"And I know you'd enjoy it," she said with a rueful smile. "But Caroline would not be happy, and it would be terrible if you were put in jail in Chicago."

"But the man deserves it!"

"I agree, but I don't want you in trouble. You have to stay home and take care of your family. Especially now that they're all home." Toby and his wife and kids were living in the big house, Josh had just graduated from college and come back to the ranch, and now Caroline had returned to Rawhide.

"Yeah. You think she'll stay?"

"I think she's going to give it a try. She dreaded telling us the truth. But she's done that. She loves the house, and I think she'll love the work."

"So there's nothing I can do?"

B.J. gave her husband a smile. "Well, you do have a specialty that might come in handy."

"What's that?"

"Matchmaking," she said with a big smile.

Chapter Two

Both her parents drove Caroline back to her house that evening after dinner. Red, who'd quickly whipped up her favorite chocolate cake, sent a big piece of it home with her in case she got hungry. She'd been kissed and hugged by every member of the Randall family. Her cousins Rich, Russ and their wives and children had come over, as had Uncle Griff and Aunt Camille. Caroline had even met cousins Nick and Gabe and their wives for the first time.

"Wow, there sure are a lot of Randalls now," she exclaimed.

"Yeah," her dad agreed.

"And lots of babies," said her mother.

At that her father seemed to blanch, as if horrified by what his wife had said.

Caroline stared straight ahead and allowed no reaction to show on her face.

"So you see," her mom continued, "we've got grandkids. Two from Toby. So do all of Dad's brothers. There's nothing to worry about."

"Okay, Mom, I get your point."

"Your mom and I would like you to stay six

months or a year before you make up your mind about whether you'll settle here. Is that asking too much?''

Just like her father to get right to the point, she thought. ''No, Dad. But I'm not making any promises. We'll see how it goes.''

''Fine. You sure you'll be all right in that house by yourself?''

''Yes. I managed to live alone in Chicago. I think I can handle Rawhide.''

''You call me if you need anything, okay?''

''Okay, Daddy.'' She kissed his cheek. Then she slid out of the truck after her mother. She gave her a hug and took the piece of chocolate cake B.J. had been holding. ''Tell Red thanks again.''

''I will, darling. And welcome home.''

''Thank you, Mom. You and Dad are the best.''

''Let's just hope Don doesn't decide to come visit you here in Rawhide. We don't want your father to be arrested.'' She kissed her daughter's cheek before she got back in the truck.

Caroline stood there waving until the truck was out of sight. Then she unlocked the door and went inside. It really was a beautiful little house. Done in primary colors, the living room boasted a red sofa, a big blue chair, and had yellow and green throw pillows scattered all around. There wasn't one fussy ruffle to be seen in the entire house.

She headed toward the kitchen with the wrapped-up piece of cake. There was no way she could eat it after Mildred's delicious dinner. Caroline supposed she could save it for another day....

But as she entered the kitchen, a sudden thought

struck her. She stepped to the phone and dialed the Sheriff's Office.

"Is Sheriff Davis there?"

"Yes, ma'am, he is," the man answering the phone said. "Just a minute."

"Wait! I don't want to—"

"Sheriff Davis." The deep voice was one she recognized.

"Sheriff, it's Caroline Randall."

"Ah. Dr. Randall."

She remembered how she'd told him her title. Regret surged through her now. "Look, I wanted to bring you something. I can—"

"I'll be at your place in about two minutes."

"No, wait!" Before she could continue, the line went dead.

Now she had the sheriff calling on her late at night. By morning half the town would know and she'd have yet another apology to make. This time to his wife.

A knock on the front door drew her attention. He'd made the trip in under two minutes. After letting him in, she closed the door and turned to him.

She hadn't noticed this morning what a big man he was. Like her daddy. There wasn't a spare ounce on him, but he had to be at least six foot four. Since she was five-eight, his size didn't intimidate her.

"You misunderstood, Sheriff. I didn't want you to come visit me."

One eyebrow slid up. "Why not?"

She shot him a disbelieving look. "How long have you been here in Rawhide?"

"Two weeks."

She gave him a superior smile. "Well, for your information, half the people in town will know about your late call. Now I'll have to contact your wife and apologize to her, too."

"No, you won't."

"Either I do that or all of them will be calling me a whore for trying to make a pass at a married man!" she snapped. "I grew up here, Sheriff. I know how this town works."

He put his hands on his hips. "Maybe you do, ma'am. I won't argue with you. But I don't happen to have a wife, so apologizing to her would be kind of hard."

Blindsided by his remark, Caroline scoured her brain for a response, but all she could manage was a pathetic "Oh."

"Now, why did you call?"

Caroline realized she'd overreacted again. He was going to think she was an idiot. "I was going to offer you a piece of Red's chocolate cake as an apology for this morning."

He waved his hand to dismiss her words. "Not necessary. You've already apologized."

Caroline sighed. "We both know I wasn't sincere. I—I was upset and I took it out on you. I really am sorry."

He gave her a warm, approving smile. "Now, that apology I'll gladly accept, ma'am." He tipped his hat, a mannerism she'd seen her father use many a time.

She turned and picked up the piece of cake. "I wish you'd take this along with the apology."

"I don't want to take it back to the office. If I do

I'll soon be flooded with cakes and pies from every unmarried woman in town.''

''Well, you're a little full of yourself, aren't you?'' She regretted her words as soon as they were out. His friendly smile disappeared.

He tipped his hat again. ''Yes, ma'am.'' Then he turned and headed for the front door.

She wanted to stop him. She wanted to force him to eat the chocolate cake. She wanted to turn back time to that morning and change her behavior. But none of that was possible. So she stood silently and watched him go out of her house, closing the door behind him.

But he didn't leave.

''Please lock up, Dr. Randall,'' he said from outside her door. He waited for her to obey him.

Not to do so would make her appear stupid, as well as rude. She hurried to the door and turned the lock. Then she crossed her arms over her chest and said briskly, ''Done, Sheriff.''

''Good night.'' She heard his footsteps fade away.

So much for her attempt to mend bridges. Mike Davis had made it clear he had no interest in how she behaved as long as it didn't affect him.

''Fine!'' she snapped, knowing he couldn't hear her. But to spite him, she sailed into the kitchen, sat down and ate every last crumb of the chocolate cake. That would show him!

MUCH TO CAROLINE'S surprise, she stayed busy all week. A number of her patients didn't need much health care; they were willing to pay her fee just to satisfy their curiosity about her.

Unfortunately, the sheriff figured in many of the probing conversations.

Caroline didn't see him at all, which seemed hard to manage in Rawhide unless it was intentional.

But that changed Friday night.

She stayed late, writing up files and reviewing the week. After all, she had no plans, other than an invitation to the Randall homestead. She figured she might go out tomorrow evening instead.

Her mind wandered, lost in thoughts about her future. The work had been satisfying, but, in addition to queries about her and the sheriff, folks had discussed her having a family. She'd simply met their deeply personal questions with a smile and moved on.

A banging on the front door and the hurried footsteps of Alice, the nurse on duty, told her they had a late customer. Caroline checked her watch and was shocked to discover it was after nine o'clock.

"Doctor?" Alice called.

Caroline stepped into the hall to see the nurse and a deputy helping Mike Davis onto a gurney. Blood seemed to be everywhere.

Tamping down any kind of personal reaction, Caroline pulled on a pair of scrubs and stepped to the patient's side. "What happened?"

"Knife fight," Mike muttered. He was obviously in pain.

Alice wheeled the gurney into the operating room while Caroline did a quick but thorough scrub. By the time she entered the sterile room Alice had removed Mike's sheepskin coat and cut away his shirt. Caroline stared at the nasty, bleeding gash across several ribs.

She cleaned the wound and anesthetized the skin. Then she began stitching it. Her patient lay perfectly still, but his eyes never wavered from her.

"You're not feeling any pain now, are you?" she asked, glancing at him in concern.

"No. But I'm wondering if you've had any experience taking care of fight wounds. I thought you worked with children."

"Are you trying to tell me men who fight with knives are adults?"

Much to her surprise, he grinned. "Maybe you've got a point. Those two tonight didn't exhibit much adult behavior."

"If you weren't the one fighting, how did you get this wound?" she asked.

"Trying to stop it."

"Oh. I think I'd ask for a raise."

He frowned. "It's not that bad, is it? Just a couple of stitches and I'll be good to go, right?"

Caroline rolled her eyes at Alice. "Men! That stiff-upper-lip stuff doesn't work on me. You lost a lot of blood. How long did it take you to get here?"

"We came right away, as soon as we locked up both fighters."

"You didn't have someone else who could do that?"

"They pay me to do my job."

"Ah, stubborn as well as macho."

She finished her stitching and clipped the thread. "Okay, Alice, get his blood type. We're going to need to give him some blood. And we'll be keeping him overnight."

"Overnight?" Mike yelped. "You've got to be kidding!"

Caroline shook her head. "I'm not kidding. You *have* lost a lot of blood." She removed and discarded her gloves. "Rawhide will just have to survive without you tonight, Sheriff."

With that, she left him in Alice's capable hands and went to her office, where she changed out of the soiled scrubs. Too bad it wasn't as easy to divest herself of her thoughts of Sheriff Davis. He reminded her so much of the men in her family. Stubborn, determined, refusing to be cosseted. He didn't look like them, though. He wasn't as rangy in build but muscular and broad. She felt herself flush just thinking about his body. She had to admit the man was sexy.

The ladies in Rawhide would work themselves into a frenzy to catch his attention. With a chuckle, she imagined the shameless efforts to attract him that would no doubt be expended by even the most timid bachelorette.

Alice tapped lightly on the open door.

"Come in, Alice. Is our patient settled?"

She grinned. "That he is. He's a charmer, too. He made it clear he didn't want to be here, but he still flashed me one of those killer smiles of his." She patted her chest. "Be still my heart."

"Alice, shame on you. You're a married lady!" Caroline teased.

"I can still look. But what's wrong with you? You're not married."

"Don't start, Alice. I have enough of that from my family."

"I guess you do at that. Your dad is a whiz at matchmaking."

"He thinks he is. I think he just does some persuading in situations that are already there. But I figure if I stay away from all men, he won't have a chance."

Alice stared at Caroline. "That may be true, Doctor, but won't you get lonesome?"

Caroline shook her head, but in truth, she was already feeling as if she were in exile from her life in Chicago. "Of course not," she replied briskly, hoping to disguise any loneliness she was already feeling. "I'll check on the sheriff now. Then I'm going home. You have my number if you have any concerns. Don't hesitate to call me."

"All right, Doctor."

"Alice, when it's just us, call me Caroline. After all, we've known each other all our lives."

"I didn't want to overstep," the nurse said with a grin.

Caroline smiled and shook her head. "That couldn't happen."

"All right, Caroline. See you in the morning." Alice returned to the nurse's station, where she could monitor the patient's condition without too much effort.

Caroline straightened her desk, making sure everything was in its place for immediate action in the morning. Back in Chicago she'd done two rotations in the ER and she knew life didn't wait for methodical preparation. If she wanted to save lives, she had to be ready at a moment's notice.

Not that tonight's emergency had been life threatening. If the sheriff had come at once, he would be home in his bed by now. But by postponing care, he had lost a lot of blood.

"Maybe he has to learn the hard way," she muttered as she gathered her medical bag and her coat and headed for the patient's room.

The night-light there illuminated his large form in the bed, covered by a sheet and blankets. She checked the IV drip before touching his wrist to take his pulse.

"Afraid I might die on you?" he murmured, barely opening his eyes.

She was surprised he'd responded at all, since Alice should have given him a mild sedative. "You're awake?"

"Unless I'm dreaming about a beautiful angel of mercy."

"Didn't the nurse give you a sedative?" Caroline asked sharply, ignoring the tingle of pleasure she felt at his compliment.

"I believe she did offer one," he said. Caroline guessed he hadn't taken the medicine, hiding that fact from Alice. She hit the call button.

"It's not her fault," the sheriff hastily said. "And it's nothing to be concerned about. I'm in charge of the town, so I have to be alert. I'll get enough sleep on my own."

Caroline looked down her nose at him. "I expect my orders to be obeyed, Sheriff Davis."

"Then you're bound to be disappointed in life, aren't you?"

She couldn't believe the sheriff was teasing her. Fortunately, Alice entered at that moment.

"Yes, Doctor?"

"Alice, it appears the sheriff did not take his sedative."

"But I watched him!" she assured her.

"I'm sure you did. Could you bring another pill, please?"

Alice left at once to carry out the order.

The sheriff tried arguing his point again. "It really isn't necessary, you know. I don't need a lot of sleep." He looked at her stubbornly, an expression she instantly recognized.

"Your body needs restorative time to recover from the loss of blood, Sheriff Davis. You have no choice."

"I've heard about doctors having a Godlike attitude, but this is the first time I've ever experienced it. Are all doctors like you?"

"Yes."

"So they're all beautiful women?"

"Sheriff—" she began.

"Make it Mike. If you're going to order me around like my mother, we might as well be informal."

She ignored him as Alice returned with a small pill in a miniature paper cup. Taking the cup, Caroline signaled that Alice could return to the nurse's desk, leaving the patient in her care. Caroline poured a glass of water, then held the pill near his lips. "Open, please."

He reached up a hand, but she drew back. "No hands," she ordered. They stared at each other in a silent struggle. Finally he opened his mouth. She dropped the pill in and then handed him the glass of water. "Drink it all," she insisted.

He did so, reluctantly. "Satisfied?" he asked.

"Yes, thank you. Sleep tight and I'll see you tomorrow."

"No good-night kiss?"

There was a challenge in his gaze that made her feel reckless. Delighting in that feeling, she bent over, intending to kiss his cheek, but he turned his head and met her lips with his.

His soft yet powerful mouth clung to hers, and Caroline was shocked at how much she wanted to give in to their touch. That very thought shocked her even more and she jerked away.

She intended to reprimand him, but she couldn't pull herself together. Instead, he murmured, "That was worth it." A sweet smile formed on his lips and he drifted off to sleep.

She backed away from the bed, as if an incredible danger lay there and could draw her in if she went too close. Her body was flooded with sensations. What was wrong with her? No man had ever done so much damage with a single kiss.

She turned and hurried down the hall.

"Everything okay, Caroline?" Alice asked, staring at her curiously.

"Yes, fine. Good night." She never stopped walking, trying desperately not to run. When she stepped outside into the cold, crisp night air, she drew a deep breath and some of her panic faded.

It was because she was tired. Because she wasn't used to being home again. Those facts were to blame for her unbridled reaction to Sheriff Mike Davis. Nothing else.

That was it, she told herself, pleased with her self-diagnosis. All she had to do was pull herself together and get a good night's sleep. Starting tomorrow she would just avoid the new sheriff.

Her house was safe and warm, comforting. But she didn't dare go to bed right away. First she needed to clear her mind of what had happened so she didn't have to relive the experience in her dreams.

After reading far too late, she finally retired to her bed and closed her eyes. Snug in the covers, her head resting on a fluffy pillow, Caroline began drifting off. But just as sleep claimed her, she found herself wrapped in Mike's arms, his lips claiming hers...and a smile formed on her lips.

HER LIPS WERE SWOLLEN and cherry-red from his sweet-tasting kisses, yet she couldn't stop herself from taking pleasure in his mouth one more time. Her tongue danced with his and—

What was that rapping sound she heard pounding in her ears? The beating of her own heart, she reasoned. Then she heard it again and this time identified it. Someone was knocking on her door.

With a start Caroline awoke and sat bolt upright in her bed. Around her the sheets lay in a twisted heap. If she didn't know better, she'd think this was the site of a long night of passionate lovemaking. Her and Mike Davis...

No. Whatever had transpired between her and Mike had happened only in he dreams.

Erasing the carnal image from her mind, she grabbed her robe and pulled it on, trying to look at her watch at the same time as she struggled to get to the front door.

"I'm coming," she called out.

When she opened the door, her mother stood there, her eyebrows raised.

"Good morning, dear. Did I awaken you?"

"Yes, but I'm glad you did. Is anything wrong?"

"No. I took an emergency call out at the Benton ranch this morning. I thought I'd stop and take you to breakfast before I went home."

"Oh. Oh, yes, that will be nice." Caroline stepped back and allowed her mom to enter. She felt strange, almost as if she didn't want to make eye contact with her mother for fear her eyes would be a life-size screen on which would play the images of her and her lover that had imprinted her dreams last night and into this morning.

"I—I'll get dressed," she said, walking toward her bedroom.

"Are you sure you're all right?"

"Of course, Mom. I won't be a minute."

In her bedroom she frantically found a pair of jeans and a knit shirt to put on, adding socks and boots. Then she ran a brush through her long hair and braided it down her back. Taking a deep breath, she came back into the living room. "I'm ready, Mom."

Her mother was sitting on the couch, looking at a magazine. "There's no big rush, Caro. At least, that's true unless Red learns we chose the café over his cooking."

Caroline relaxed a little. "Do you mind if we stop by the clinic? I need to check on a patient before we go."

"Of course not, dear. Who's the patient? Anyone I know?"

Caroline made sure she was turned away so her

mother wouldn't see any undue emotion in her face. "Sheriff Davis. He got cut breaking up a fight last night."

Her mother frowned. "Must've been a bad cut to require overnight care."

"It shouldn't have been, but he insisted on taking the men to jail before he came in. He lost a lot of blood."

"Ah. One of those stubborn men."

"Exactly. Not only did he not want to stay in the hospital, but he also faked taking his sedative. I had to give it to him personally to ensure that he swallowed it."

Her mom laughed. "I'm sure you managed, sweetheart. You've always been a strong woman."

It was comforting to think her mother believed in her. But memories of the initial confusion and desire to yield to Mike Davis's touch worried Caroline. That was why she asked her mother to accompany her into his room when they reached the clinic.

The man wouldn't be able to get to her with her mother present.

Caroline greeted the nurse on duty, who had relieved Alice at seven. "Morning, Helen. How's our patient this morning?"

"If you mean the sheriff, he signed out just after I came on board this morning. Said he didn't need any more care. I tried to convince him to wait until you arrived, but he refused."

"Why didn't you call me?" Caroline asked sternly.

"Sorry, Doctor. I didn't think it would be necessary to disturb you."

"Did he say where he was going?"

"He'd called one of his deputies and said he was going to the café for breakfast."

"I see," Caroline said, biting her tongue. Then she turned to her mother. "Let's go there and see if I can find my missing patient!"

Chapter Three

"Uh-oh," Mike Davis muttered as he watched the newest arrivals enter the café. Dr. Caroline Randall stared around the room until her blue gaze collided with his.

"What, boss?" Harry Gowan asked before he put a big bite of scrambled eggs in his mouth.

"I think I've irritated the doctor."

"Jon? How—"

"The new one, Dr. Randall," Mike said, watching as the beautiful woman cut through the tables of diners. He could tell she was going to challenge his behavior.

Harry's eyes widened as he noted her approach, followed by that of B.J. Randall, of the all-powerful Randall family. "Uh, boss, that's Mrs. Randall."

"I know." He stood and addressed the women. "Good morning, Doctor, Mrs. Randall. Would you join us? We've just started."

B.J. accepted the offer without consulting her daughter. Caroline found herself face-to-face with the sheriff while her mother sat down beside the handsome young deputy.

Mike pulled out the chair beside him and gestured for Caroline to sit down. Without causing a scene that would hurriedly be repeated on Rawhide's grapevine, Caroline had no choice. She flashed a look of panic at her mother, but the woman was discussing something trivial with the deputy and didn't glance her way.

"I assume you're upset that I signed myself out?" the sheriff asked in a low tone meant only for her ears.

"I thought it was an unprofessional thing to do," she said stiffly.

Before Mike could reply, a voice interrupted them. "Hey, Caro! I heard you were back. Why did it take so long for you to come in?" the waitress asked as she reached their table.

Caroline wanted to sink down in her chair, but she smiled brightly. "Hey, Sylvia. It's good to see you. But I've been busy since I got in. I started work at once."

"Well, your first breakfast is on the house. What will you have?"

Caroline gave her order. Then she sat quietly as her mother did the same.

After the waitress departed, Mike leaned forward. "I was going to offer to buy your breakfast, but since it's on the house, I guess I won't bother."

"You wouldn't need to do so, anyway. Are you going to check in sometime today so I can examine the wound?" She held her breath for his answer.

"I already examined it. It's not the first knife wound I've had."

"And that makes you an expert?"

"How many such wounds have you treated? I don't think many upper-crust Chicagoans get knife wounds." He gave her his charming smile.

"Sheriff Davis, I did two ER rotations. I can assure you knife wounds were commonplace."

Mike frowned, staring at her. "You dealt with the ER? That's pretty tough."

"Yes, it was. But I happen to be pretty tough myself. I'd like you to come to the clinic sometime today for me to check the wound."

He paused before he answered. "What time?"

"I'll be at the clinic all day after I finish breakfast. Jon and I are going to alternate Saturdays. Today's my turn. On Sundays we'll only have a couple of nurses on duty."

"Darling, I'm sorry," her mother interrupted. "I didn't realize you hadn't met Harry. This is Deputy Harry Gowan. Harry, my daughter, Caroline."

"Or Dr. Randall, as she's known to some people," Mike added, eyeing Caroline.

She blushed, remembering her snippy remark, which she now regretted. "'Caroline' will be fine, Harry. Rawhide is a friendly town."

"It sure is, Caroline. Welcome home."

"Thank you. How long have you lived here?"

"Three years now. Sheriff Metzger hired me right out of college. I wasn't sure what I wanted to do and he promised me some excitement."

The deputy seemed very young to Caroline. Probably twenty-five, from what he'd said, which gave her five years on him. "And you, Sheriff Davis? Were you hired straight from college?"

"No, ma'am. I didn't make it to college."

"Oh?" Since she'd gone to school for what felt like her whole lifetime, the idea of Mike not attending college seemed bizarre.

"I joined the army. Afterwards I worked with the Chicago PD for ten years."

Quickly she did the mental calculations to figure out his age.

As if reading her mind, Mike offered, "I'm thirty-five."

Unconsciously, Caroline let go a sigh of relief. Otherwise, she would've thought she'd robbed the cradle when he'd kissed her last night.

She recovered quickly and shrugged it off. "Yes, well, I'm sure you learned a great deal while working."

He smiled wryly. "Yeah. Quite a bit."

"He's great," Harry said with enthusiasm. "I've learned a lot since he got here. Not that I'm saying anything against Sheriff Metzger," Harry hurriedly added, looking apologetically at Mike.

"Thanks, Harry. When I start campaigning for election next year, I'll enlist you as my PR guy."

Just then Sylvia brought the ladies' food. Mike looked at Caroline's plate. "That's a big breakfast," he commented.

"I have a fast metabolism," she said, not looking at him.

"Say, Caroline, are you planning on staying here?" the young deputy asked, obviously trying to make polite conversation.

"I'm not sure, Harry. I'm going to work with Jon for a while and see how I like it." She smiled at the pleasant man.

"Afraid you'll miss the sophistication of Chicago?" Mike asked.

"No. Are you?"

"Not me. I never went to the symphony or the ballet."

"But I bet you went to football, basketball and baseball games occasionally. We don't have those here in Rawhide."

He grinned and raised that left eyebrow. "No, but the high school has a great wrestling program. And the basketball team is getting better."

"I heard you're helping coach the basketball team," B.J. said. "My nephew Casey has been raving about you."

Caroline looked at her mother. "Casey is playing basketball?"

"He's good," Mike said. "And a hard worker."

"I'll tell Pete you said so. That will make him proud," B.J. said.

"But he's all arms and legs." Caroline couldn't get the image of the gangly teen from her mind. "He seemed so awkward when I saw him last time."

Mike looked at B.J., not Caroline. "Beautiful women do that to young men." He winked at her mother, who laughed in appreciation. "When he gets on the court, though, he makes good use of his talents."

"And you're doing this as a part-time job?" Caroline asked.

"Volunteer work. It helps keep me in shape."

"But you won't be playing for a couple of weeks at least," she said in her doctorly voice.

"Maybe one week."

"Sheriff, as your doctor, I certainly wouldn't approve of you testing your wound that soon."

He smiled. "I heal quickly."

Caroline saw his comment as a challenge to her authority and glared at him. She wiped her mouth with her napkin and stood up. "I need to be going, Mother. Harry, I'm glad I met you. Sheriff, I'll see you for your checkup today." With a nod, she was gone.

B.J. sat there, surprise on her face.

"Sorry to drive your daughter away, Mrs. Randall." Mike spoke sincerely, but his lips were curved in a rueful smile.

"Make it B.J., Mike. There are too many Mrs. Randalls in Rawhide. And I'm sure you didn't drive Caroline away. She's just determined to do her job well."

"I'm sure she will."

When the waitress brought the bill, Mike took it, insisting on paying for Harry's and B.J.'s breakfasts. Then he headed to the clinic, ready to get closer to Caroline Randall again.

CAROLINE ENTERED an examination room and extended a hand to greet an old high school friend. "Tracey, I'm so glad to see you. How are you?"

"Fine, Caroline. We're glad you're back in town. Jon was overrun with patients."

"He must've been because we're both working hard." Then Caroline bent down to greet the two children accompanying her friend. "Hello. Who is Beth and who is Jenny?"

The girls, eight and five, shyly identified themselves. Caroline noticed the younger one, Jenny, was flushed, and she rang for a nurse. "Let's check the temps," she suggested, still smiling. Then she turned to Tracey. "What symptoms have they been showing?"

"Colds, I thought, but they keep hanging on. It's right before Christmas vacation, so I've sent them to school. But we're supposed to go to Denver for Christmas with my parents, and I don't want to give anything to Mom and Dad."

"You haven't had any of the symptoms?"

She didn't know if Tracey's look of sheer exhaustion was from an illness or from being run ragged taking care of two young kids.

Her friend dropped her gaze. "Well, I've gotten tired lately, but it's because I'm trying to get ready for Christmas, I think."

"Why don't we give you a little checkup, too? Take both girls into the bathroom and all three of you give us a sample."

After ten minutes, Caroline diagnosed the girls with infected throats and fever. She prescribed antibiotics for both of them, bed rest and a lot of fluids. Then she turned to her friend. "Tracey, you're run-down. Maybe you should take some iron pills."

Before she could reply, the nurse came in and handed Caroline a note. After glancing at it, Caroline asked the nurse to take the girls to pick out the color of lollipop they wanted for being so good.

As soon as the little girls left, she asked her friend to sit down. "I have some news for you, Tracey."

"The girls? It's worse than you thought?" she asked anxiously.

"No. It's about you. And I hope it's good news. You're pregnant."

Tracey paled and Caroline reached for her, afraid she might pass out.

"No!" Tracey cried.

Caroline backed her into a chair before she answered, "I gather it's not good news?"

"No! I mean—I've made plans. Next fall, when both girls are in school all day, I was going to get a job, try to get rid of some of the debt. Maybe…maybe get a divorce."

Caroline gave herself a moment before she responded. "Why? Tracey, what's wrong?"

Her friend looked away. "M-my husband gets violent when he's been drinking."

"He hits you?"

Tracey nodded.

"I don't see any bruises."

"I've been locking the three of us in the girls' room. He's given up trying to get in, and sleeps it off. In the morning he's sorry." She looked at Caroline. "But it's usually only on Friday nights."

Caroline kept any censure from her voice. "Have you tried to get him help?"

Tracy shook her head. "It would embarrass him."

"I see. Well, I'd like to examine you today."

Tracey nodded and stood up compliantly. "I'm still taking birth control pills. Will that hurt the baby?"

"I hope not. We'll watch it closely. And of course, you need to stop taking them at once."

After the examination, Caroline said, "Everything appears normal. I think you're about two months along." Smiling, she told her friend goodbye, wishing she could wave a magic wand to make the new baby a happy event. But she couldn't.

Her mind was still on Tracy when she found the sheriff in the next room. She barely greeted him. Telling him to lie down, she rang for a nurse. "Please open the sheriff's shirt so I can look at the wound." After examining it, Caroline spread a topical antibiotic cream on the cut and then bandaged it. "Please leave this bandage on and don't get the area wet for a week."

Then she sent the nurse away. "Sheriff, do we have many cases of wife beating?" she asked abruptly.

Frowning as he sat up and buttoned his shirt, Mike said, "Not since I've been here. Do you know of any, or have suspicions?"

She looked away and shook her head.

"Caroline? Are you sure?"

"I—I'm not certain."

"Let me know if you do. I'll try to improve the situation."

She nodded. From the tension in her body and the look on her face, she knew he could tell she was still worried. But she couldn't help it. She feared for her friend and the two little girls.

Mike stood and tucked in his shirt. Then he reached out and cupped her chin. "You can't change the world, Doc. Just do what you can."

Much to her surprise, she found his touch a comfort. She nodded, grateful for his reassurances and his advice. Then Mike left the room, leaving her alone with her thoughts and fears.

They were her constant companions all day. No

matter what patient she saw, Tracey remained on her mind.

Her fears turned prophetic at nine that night when her home phone rang.

"Doctor, we have an emergency with a patient you saw today. Tracey Long."

"I'll be right there."

Caroline grabbed her coat and flew out the door. Usually the walk took her a couple of minutes. Now she reached the clinic door in about thirty seconds. She could already guess what had happened. She found Tracey cleaned and prepped for examination, but Caroline winced at the angry bruises on her friend's slim body.

"Tracey, did your husband do this?"

The woman nodded.

"Where are the girls? Are they okay?"

"They're sleeping. He…didn't touch them. But, Caroline, I—I think I lost the baby." She ended with a sob.

Reassuring her friend, Caroline started her examination, but told the nurse to summon the sheriff at once. Wide-eyed, Alice hurried from the room.

After the examination, Caroline determined that the baby was indeed lost. In addition Tracey's arm was broken, and she had several painful bruises and cuts. Caroline had the nurse give Tracey a sedative that would put her to sleep right away.

"Transfer her to a long-term care room," Caroline told Alice. "She'll be staying for several days, at least. Is the sheriff here yet?"

"Yes," Alice assured her. "He's in the waiting room."

Caroline nodded and pulled off her gloves. She went out to the waiting room.

Mike stood as soon as she entered. "You okay?" he asked quickly.

"Me?" She looked down at the blood on her clothes. "Oh, yes. But I need you to arrest Jerry Long for murder."

"Murder?" Instantly Mike's face tightened and his back straightened. He went into sheriff mode. "Who's the victim?"

"It's an unborn infant. He beat his wife and caused a miscarriage."

Without saying anything, Mike turned to go.

"Wait. I'm coming with you."

"Why?"

"Because they have two little girls. I have to make sure they're all right."

"Okay. Get changed."

She hurried into her office and changed into a pair of clean scrubs, then grabbed her coat.

Mike was hanging up the phone when she returned. Without a word, he led the way outside to his SUV. "One of my deputies will meet us there."

On the short drive, he asked, "This is the woman that made you ask a question about wife-beaters, isn't it?"

Caroline nodded, fighting to hold back tears.

Outside the Long house the deputy was waiting in his car. He got out when he saw the sheriff do so, and Caroline joined them. Mike knocked on the door after telling her to hang back until they'd determined what was going on. "Sheriff! Open up!" he yelled.

At first, there was no response. Then they heard

movement. Finally the door swung open and Tracey's husband, obviously drunk, glared at them. "What's a'matter?"

"Jerry Long, you're under arrest for assaulting your wife and causing the death of your unborn child." Mike didn't wait for his response. He whirled him around and had him cuffed before Jerry could rise out of his drunken stupor.

As soon as the cuffs were on, Caroline pushed past the men and hurried into the house. She found both children asleep in their beds, unharmed and unaware of what had happened.

She woke them up gently, telling them that their mommy was sick and in the hospital, and they were going to spend the night at Caroline's house. She told them to put on their coats over their nightgowns, and gathered up clothes for the morning.

Mike appeared at the bedroom door. "I've sent—the deputy is taking care of the other issue," he said cryptically so as not to alert the children. "Where are you taking them?"

"To my house. I have a guest room."

"Okay. I'll drive you three there." He knelt and tied Jenny's tennis shoes for her. "Hi, I'm Mike. What's your name?"

"Jenny," the child said, shying away from him.

"Mike is the sheriff," Caroline said. "He keeps us safe."

Mike introduced himself to Beth. Then he offered to carry them to his car. Much to Caroline's surprise, both girls allowed him to lift them in his arms.

"I can carry one of them," she said.

"Your job is to open doors for us, right, girls?" he said with a smile.

Beth agreed, while Jenny giggled and clung to his neck. Caroline nodded and proceeded to do her duty.

When they reached her house, Mike carried the girls again, following Caroline inside.

"I'll make some cocoa for all of us, so the girls can get back to sleep," Caroline said.

She got busy in the kitchen while Mike took the children into the living room. While they drank their cocoa, Mike told them stories about a dog named Chipper. Both girls suddenly wanted a dog.

Then he carried them to the big bed in Caroline's guest room, where Caroline tucked them in and kissed them good night.

They stepped out of the room and Caroline gestured to the living area. After they sat down, she said, "You were very good with the children. Thank you."

"No problem."

"Can we make the charges stick?" she asked, cutting to her main concern.

"Depends. I'll call Nick Randall in the morning. Once Jerry sobers up and makes bail, I don't know about keeping him behind bars."

"This isn't the first time he's hit her. But she said it's usually only on Friday night. I guess she told him about the baby, and that might have set him off. But when did he have time to get drunk?"

"I'll investigate tomorrow," Mike promised.

"I wish I'd told you earlier today."

"I understand that you couldn't betray a patient's trust."

''But the baby—'' She broke off, realizing she was losing control.

Mike left his seat and stepped forward, bending down to wrap his arms around her. ''I know, honey, but you did what you could.''

''It wasn't enough!'' she complained as tears flowed from her eyes.

''It never is,'' he said sadly. ''But we can't control the world. We just have to do what we can to pick up the pieces.''

He rocked her against him, dropping several kisses on her brow. She looked up and his lips covered hers, as they had last night, but this time, in her weakened emotional state, her response was more intense. As if of their own accord her arms wrapped around his neck, and she pressed her breasts against him.

Mike deepened the kiss. His embrace made her feel weak and protected, almost loved. Of course, it was an illusion, she reminded herself, even as she welcomed their closeness. Tonight had shaken her badly. When she wanted a baby more than anything, to see one thrown away, as Jerry Long had done, was tragic. She sought solace in his kiss.

She found so much more.

Mike's lips left hers and trailed a hot path across her jaw and down her neck to the pulse point that pounded due to her suddenly rapid heartbeat. He feasted on her sensitive flesh, and she felt herself come alive. All over, her body seemed to sing out for his touch, for his wet kisses.

Mike took her lips again, hard and demanding. His tongue plundered her mouth, urging a response. And Caroline answered him.

Then, without warning, he pulled away. "Caroline, we can't do this."

She felt bereft, and longed to draw him close again. "Mike," she said on a ragged breath, "what's wrong?"

For a few seconds he said nothing, then finally murmured, "I can't keep kissing you. It's not enough for me." His hazel eyes met her blue ones. "And I can't lose control. Not with you. I know you don't want more than this."

Even as she shook her head, her heart was screaming, *Yes!* She wanted more than this, all right. She wanted all of Mike Davis. But she couldn't tell him. Instead, she dropped her arms at her sides and said, "I'm sorry, Mike. It's just that I was so upset…"

He seemed to gather himself right before her eyes. "Well, then," he said after he cleared his throat and put on his hat, "I'll go back to the office and make sure everything's set there. You'll be all right with the girls?"

"Yes. I'll be fine. They'll sleep until morning, I'm sure. And I don't work tomorrow. Jon is on call."

"Good. I'll check with you in the morning."

She followed him to the door—to lock it, of course, after his departure, she told herself. But when he bent his head and placed a gentle kiss on her cheek, she didn't back away. Then he straightened and said, "Lock up." Touching her cheek, he strode out the door and stood there looking at her.

It took her a minute to realize he was waiting for her to follow his order. She tried to give a brisk nod, but she wasn't sure she could pull it off. Instead she shut the door, turned the lock. He softly called good-night through the door and she heard his footsteps fading away.

She was alone.

Chapter Four

Mike's first thought the next morning was of Caroline…and the girls. He was the only one on duty, so the other men could attend church. When one of them came in at noon, he'd be free to check on his favorite doctor.

He shook his head at the thought. He couldn't go to her. Not with his intentions. Caroline Randall was out of his league and he'd best remember it. Not only was she a doctor, but she was also one of the wealthy Randalls. While Rawhide paid a good sheriff's salary, he supposed because so many wealthy ranchers contributed to it, it would never match Caroline's resources.

He'd sat up all night, thinking of her, reliving their kiss, planning the next time they could be alone together. Around dawn, he'd come to his senses.

He was successful, all right, and proud of what he'd made of himself, of his life. As proud of what he'd become as what he'd overcome. Raised by a single mother after his father died when he was a young boy, he'd worked hard for whatever he'd gained. Thank God for Uncle Bill, he thought. The man had helped out whenever he could. But it had been the promise of a secure job and a steady paycheck—not to mention the self-esteem—that had lured Mike to the army a couple of years after high school. After having been an M.P., he'd considered the jump to the police force a natural one after the military.

Throughout his life, no one had ever handed anything to Mike Davis. Not even his job. He'd worked to distinguish himself in the Chicago PD, to build an untarnished record of service that made him a viable choice to succeed Bill as sheriff of Rawhide.

It was that same tenaciousness and righteousness that forced him to see how wrong he was for Caroline Randall. How they could never have anything but a secret dalliance. And wasn't it she who'd said nothing was ever secret in this town?

No, he'd just have to stay away from her—socially, anyway.

He'd check on her and the children because he'd said he would. But that was it. Doing his duty. That was all he'd do.

The phone rang. "Sheriff's Office," he said briskly, trying to erase his thoughts about Caroline.

"Mike? Is that you?"

Mike recognized the voice. "Yes, Mr. Randall. How may I help you?"

"You the only one on duty?"

"Yes, sir. I can call in some men if I need to."

"No, not necessary. Are you being relieved at noon?"

Mike was becoming a little irritated because Jake Randall hadn't yet told him what was wrong. "Yes, Mr. Randall. But if you'll tell me the problem—"

"Sorry, son, I didn't mean to mislead you. There's no problem. We just wanted to ask you to join us for Sunday dinner about one o'clock."

Mike was pleased to be welcomed so warmly into the community, but Caroline wouldn't be happy about this invitation. "Uh, Mr. Randall, that's very nice of you, but I don't want to put anyone to any trouble."

"No trouble, boy. But you can do me a favor. I was going to go by and pick up Caroline. Could you bring her for me? She'll show you where to go."

"Of course I will, if that's what she wants. But she has two children with her. Will it be okay if they come?"

"Children? Whose children?"

"One of her patients. Tracey Long. I believe she and Caroline went to high school together."

"I'll call Caro. But if you don't hear from me, pick up her and the kids at twelve-thirty, and we'll all dine together."

"Yes, sir." Mike hung up the phone, wondering what Caroline's reaction would be.

Probably he shouldn't have accepted the invitation, because he suspected it would upset her, but he needed to get to know the people he served. Besides, his uncle had had a special relationship with the Randalls.

If Mike kept his hands off Caroline, maybe she wouldn't object to his presence. She hadn't objected last night, his inner voice reminded him. And it was true. Until he'd cautioned her about continuing.

"Big mouth!" he muttered to himself. Then she'd immediately shown him the door. It had been cold outside, but no colder than his heart as he'd heard her reject him.

"That's because you have no business starting anything with Caroline Randall. And Jake Randall will be the first one to tell you that."

Mike piddled with some paperwork, staying beside the phone, sure Caroline would call and tell him she didn't need him to pick her up. The phone rang three times, and each time he expected to hear her sexy voice. Instead, he turned down two invitations to Sunday dinner, one from a rancher and his family on the outskirts of town, and another from a widow down the street.

"I appreciate the invite, Mrs. Dunster, but I've already accepted an invitation. It's thoughtful of you to offer, though."

"I bet it was from those Randalls! They not only gobble up all the land, but they also trap all the single men for their girls! It's not fair."

"I think they're just being neighborly, ma'am."

"Humph! We'll see."

When Mike hung up the phone, he laughed. The widow didn't seem to realize any of the Randall women could manage to find suitors on their own. They were all very attractive, not to mention they had a lot of money.

When twelve o'clock arrived and one of the deputies came in to relieve him, Mike told him where he could be found in case of an emergency.

"Hey! You'd better watch out. You'll be married before you know it. The Randalls like to matchmake."

''And that's a problem?'' Mike asked with a grin. ''I haven't seen any ugly Randalls.''

The deputy nodded, grinning in turn. ''Good point, but just remember you said you didn't intend to marry.''

''I will.''

Mike hurried upstairs to the apartment the town provided over the jail. He washed up and added a corduroy jacket to his jeans and shirt to keep the chill out, then pulled on his sheepskin coat.

Climbing into his SUV, he drove the short distance to Caroline's house.

He knocked on the door, eager to see her.

But when she opened the door, her first words weren't welcoming. ''Dad said you'd be here at twelve-thirty!'' she snapped, purposely looking at her watch.

''I came early because I thought you'd want to visit your patient before we went to the ranch. I didn't think the girls should—I thought they might be bored.''

He'd changed his statement because he'd caught sight of two little faces watching him. ''Hi, girls! Did you sleep good?''

''Yeah, and Caroline made us pancakes for breakfast,'' Beth said adoringly.

''Did she? Wonderful. Did you save me some?''

Jenny didn't realize he was teasing. ''Oh, no! Are you hungry?''

He swung her up into his arms. ''No, sweetheart, I've already had breakfast.'' Then he looked at Caroline. ''Are you going to go check on your patient?''

''Yes, thank you. Girls, I'll be right back.''

When she'd left, he gathered both girls on the sofa for another Chipper story.

Before he could begin, Beth said, "Caroline's going to see Mommy. She's her patient. Do you think Mommy will be all right?"

Mike gave her a rueful smile. "I'm sure she will be. Dr. Caroline is a good doctor. You're feeling better, aren't you?"

"Yes. She gave us medicine," Beth assured him.

"And orange juice," Jenny added.

"See, I told you she was a good doctor. Now, did I tell you about when Chipper ran away from home?"

He had their attention for the next twenty minutes.

Caroline came in just as he ended the story. Both girls jumped down from the sofa and ran to her. "How's Mommy?" Beth asked. Jenny didn't speak, but her wide-eyed gaze was fixed on Caroline's face.

Caroline shot him a questioning look and he shrugged his shoulders. Then she looked at the girls. "Mommy is doing much better. After school tomorrow you can visit with her."

Both children were excited about that. Caroline told them to go put on their shoes and they would all go to lunch at her family's house.

Jenny immediately brought her shoes to Mike. He helped her, so she beat her sister in the race to get ready. Beth complained, but Caroline assured her it didn't matter.

Mike and Caroline each took a child and strapped her in the back seat. As Caroline slid into the front and attached her own seat belt, she said, "I'm sorry you got roped in by my father."

Mike raised his eyebrows. "Roped in? I thought I was accepting an invitation to lunch."

"Don't be naive, Mike. Besides, you probably would've received a number of invitations instead of providing taxi service for us."

"I did receive some invitations. Mrs. Dunster, in fact, seemed particularly put out that I was already engaged."

"Margie Dunster? She's got to be fifty, way too old for you."

"Thanks for the warning."

"I shouldn't have said anything. Actually, she may have been wanting to meet you because she was a…a particular friend of Sheriff Metzger."

Mike was a little surprised by Caroline's implication, but he only nodded.

"Turn here," she said abruptly, pointing to a gravel road that led off the county road. He did so, but there was no sign of buildings.

"How far?" he asked.

"Just a couple of miles."

He checked on his passengers in the back seat. "Are you two okay back there?"

"Yes, Mike," Beth called. Jenny smiled.

Mike smiled in return. They were sweet girls.

Lowering her voice, Caroline said, "I think Tracey is going to take them to Denver permanently. She can find work there and her mother will help take care of the girls."

"That's a good idea. Rawhide is too small for people to avoid each other all the time."

Before Caroline could answer, they topped a hill

and he saw all the buildings on the Randall ranch. "Quite a layout. How many people live here?"

"The four original brothers and their wives, my brother Josh, my half brother, Toby, and his wife, Elizabeth. Jim and his new wife, Patience, and her mother. Red and Mildred, and all the single cousins. And that doesn't include the hands. They have eight cowboys in the winter, but they hire more in the spring. Sometimes the rest of the family comes for Sunday dinner."

"The rest of the family?"

"Well, you know Jon and Tori. There's my cousin Russ and his wife and little girl. He's Tori's partner in the accounting and investment firm. And Russ's brother Rich, and Sam, his wife, and their little boy, plus she's expecting a baby after Christmas. Griff and Camille have their own place. He's Dad's cousin. They have two kids, but they're about grown. And there are cousins Nick and Gabe and their families."

Mike wouldn't be able to keep any of them straight. "I didn't think people had families that big anymore. At least in one town."

Caroline shrugged. "I never thought about that, but then, I'm so used to the crowd. What about your family? All Dad said was that you're alone here in Rawhide."

He nodded. "I have two sisters, but I left them behind in Chicago. My mother and her second husband live in Florida. So I guess, yes, I'm alone." It really never seemed to bother him; he had his work and he was committed to the people of Rawhide.

"What about your father?" she asked.

"He died when I was young."

"I'm sorry. Anyway, for today, you can share my family. There's enough to go around."

"Thanks. But I do have one question—how big is your table? It would have to be huge to fit everybody."

She smiled. "Usually they feed the children before the adults. They'll probably make all the single cousins eat with the babies today."

"You and me? We're single."

"Yes, we are, but you're a guest. You'll eat with the adults. But don't worry. They'll have enough food. Red always cooks plenty."

Mike grinned. "You had me worrying there."

"No need to worry," Caroline assured him. "You'll be in good hands."

CAROLINE HOPED HER FATHER was punishing her for her rudeness to Mike. If that wasn't his purpose, she suspected he was playing another game at which he excelled: Matchmaking. But she hoped she was wrong.

They were warmly welcomed when they arrived. Jake met Mike at the door, shaking his hand and then escorting him around, introducing him to the numerous Randalls.

Caroline tried to keep an eye on her father, but she was helping Beth and Jenny to relax and enjoy themselves.

"These little girls are darling," B.J. said.

"Yes, they are. I think they'll be moving to Denver this week, but they don't know that yet."

"How is their mother?"

"Tracey's improving, but she's going to need some

time before she can do much. I think her parents are coming tomorrow.'' Caroline watched as her father put a hand on Mike's shoulder.

Her sister-in-law, Elizabeth, approached. ''This is good for Davy.''

Caroline looked around for her four-year-old nephew. ''What is?'' she asked.

''Not being the oldest of the children. Beth is twice his age and the other children look at her as the leader. He was pouting at being supplanted, but I pulled him aside to try to improve his attitude,'' she added with a laugh.

''I hope their visiting doesn't cause any problems,'' Caroline said, distracted by her father's laugh rising above the buzz of conversation.

''No, it won't.''

''Oh, Mom,'' Caroline called as her mother started to move away.

''Yes, dear?''

''I'll eat with the children, so Beth and Jenny will be comfortable.''

''No, dear. That's not necessary. We've got everything organized. And after they eat, we have a new Disney movie for them to watch. You'll be eating in the dining room.'' With that final pronouncement her mother walked away.

Caroline looked at Elizabeth. ''Are they matchmaking?''

''You know it,'' her sister-in-law said with a smile. ''But they're giving you a choice.''

''A choice? What do you mean?''

Elizabeth leaned closer. ''They invited the new accountant Tori and Russ hired recently.''

"But I thought he was young, just out of school for a year."

Elizabeth shrugged her shoulders. "I guess they don't mind if you rob the cradle. Or there's the sheriff. He's sexy, isn't he?"

"Elizabeth! What would Toby say if he heard you?"

The other woman smiled. "Nothing. He knows I don't have any complaints."

"You're still happy?" Caroline asked softly. In addition to being married to her half brother, Toby, Elizabeth was her closest cousin, Uncle Chad and Aunt Megan's daughter. The sister she'd never had.

"Oh, yes," Elizabeth said. "He's a wonderful husband and an even better father. I'm very lucky."

Caroline squeezed her hand. "Yes, you are, and I'm glad."

"Your dad just wants the same for you."

Caroline rolled her eyes. "And if I don't want the same thing?"

"Come on, Caroline. Having someone to share your life with is important." Elizabeth stared at her, concern on her face.

"I don't want—"

They were interrupted by Toby. "Come on, ladies. We're being told to take our seats."

"But the kids are just starting to eat," Caroline pointed out.

"I know, but we're eating in the dining room," he explained.

Toby took her arm and his wife's to guide them. Once they entered the dining room, he led Caroline directly to an empty chair between the accountant and Mike.

"How do you know this is where I'm supposed to sit?" she whispered to her brother.

"Because Dad told me," he said with an apologetic smile. "It's just for dinner, sis. You'll survive."

She glared at him, but she really didn't blame him. Her father could be very persuasive. She'd hoped Toby would at least be sitting near her, but no such luck. He and Elizabeth sat on the other side of the table near the end.

Mike leaned toward her. "I thought maybe you were eating with the kids."

"No, of course not. I'm playing the role of the fatted calf," she assured him bitterly.

Mike stared at her, a question in his gaze, but she turned to the man on her right.

"Mr. Olsen, I understand you're new to Rawhide. When did you arrive?"

"I've been here four months."

"How do you like the town?" she asked. Before her companion could answer, her father stood to ask the blessing.

When Jake sat down again, Alex Olsen replied, "Rawhide is nice, but the nightlife is a little slow."

"And have you met the sheriff?"

"No, I haven't."

Caroline sat back in her chair. "Mike, this is Alex Olsen, an accountant who works for Tori and Russ."

Mike extended his hand to the other man in front of Caroline. "Glad to meet you, Alex. Mike Davis. I've only been here a couple of weeks, but I'm trying to get to know all the citizens."

The man shifted his gaze away from Mike. "Well, I try to steer clear of the law."

Caroline stared at the accountant. She hoped he wasn't being intentionally rude. "I find Mike to be good company," she said in his defense.

"I appreciate that vote of confidence, Caroline." Mike shot her one of his killer smiles.

She felt tingles all the way to her toes. Afraid she'd embarrass herself, she hurriedly looked away. "Alex is looking for nightlife in Rawhide."

Mike shrugged. "There's not much except for Friday nights, when all the cowboys pile into the steak house. There's a better selection in Buffalo."

"Really?" Alex asked eagerly.

Mike seemed to be watching him closely. "Yeah. 'Course, you need to take a designated driver along unless you want to be arrested for DWI. Or get a hotel room in Buffalo."

Alex stared at Mike. "You're kidding, right?"

Mike shook his head. "Why would I be kidding? Driving while intoxicated is dangerous and it's against the law."

"So you're worried I might mess up a fence or something?"

The man's attitude reminded Caroline of her own attitude when she'd first met the sheriff. Now it made her feel very uncomfortable.

Mike didn't lose his temper. "Strangely enough, I'm concerned about anyone being killed, including yourself. Besides, the cleanup is hell." He smiled at the man, but there was a hint of steel that again reminded Caroline of her father.

"Has Buffalo grown a lot in the past few years? I

haven't been there in ages.'' She hoped her question would change the subject.

Mike gave her a look that said he knew what she was doing, but he cooperated. ''It's a fair-size city now. They even have a French restaurant.''

''Really? Is it any good?'' Caroline asked with more enthusiasm than she'd normally show.

''So I've heard. How about I take you there for dinner one night? You can see for yourself.'' Mike kept that easy smile on his face.

''That would be—''

''French cuisine isn't a novelty for most people.'' Alex broke in, a note of sarcasm in his tone.

Caroline didn't wait for Mike to respond. ''Neither is rudeness, unfortunately!'' She hoped her words would stop the man from any more jabs. After dinner she intended to speak with her mother to ensure Mr. Olsen wouldn't frequent the Randall table.

''I'm not the one who's threatening to arrest someone,'' Alex retorted.

Mike opened his mouth to speak, but Caroline beat him to it. ''I didn't hear any threats. Just a friendly warning that you'd be wise to heed.''

Megan, who was seated on the other side of Alex, picked the perfect moment to ask him a question. Caroline suspected her aunt had been following their conversation.

She breathed a sigh of relief.

''I've been known to defend myself without starting a fight,'' Mike whispered, leaning close to her.

She sank her teeth into her bottom lip, trying to come up with a reasonable response. ''Randalls don't like their guests to be attacked. Either Mr. Olsen learns that rule or he won't be dining here again.''

"Ah. So it wasn't me you were protecting, but the pride of the Randalls? Well, you did a mighty fine job. All the more reason to treat you to dinner at the French restaurant in Buffalo.''

His hazel eyes seemed to be dancing with amusement.

"If anything, *I* should take *you* to Buffalo for dinner. When we first met, I was as obnoxious as Alex.''

"Yes, you were, and I accept your offer,'' Mike agreed, surprising her. "When are we going?''

Caroline realized he'd accepted her invitation and made it impossible for her to renege. If he were taking her, she could've done so. He was a lot smarter than the accountant.

"How about tomorrow night? Unless you have to work late?''

He grinned at her. "I think I can wrangle a free night. Will you pick me up at seven?''

Now she was thoroughly trapped. At least it would be over quickly. Twenty-four hours and then she could ignore the man.

"Yes, seven,'' she agreed. Thanks to Alex Olsen, she'd been unable to remain cold to both men. She'd have to make sure that tomorrow night she didn't let down her guard.

Those hazel eyes danced again, as if the sheriff read her mind.

Chapter Five

All day Monday, Caroline found herself thinking about her ''date'' with Mike that night. She knew it was a mistake, because she was way too fascinated by the man. And it was a fascination that would only lead to heartache. She already knew any relationship with Mike Davis—or any other man, for that matter— would die a premature death. She would never marry. To her it didn't matter if a man said he didn't want children. There'd come a time when he'd change his mind. And that was the time their marriage would end.

For that reason she'd stay single. She didn't want her heart broken.

That thought made her stop and think. She'd believed her heart was broken when Don had married his pregnant nurse. So why had the thought been of the future?

Because you never really loved Don, an inner voice said. They'd gotten along, had understood each other's hectic schedules. But that was all that was between them, she realized.

Now she wouldn't have him even if he were served

up on a gold platter. She knew his true worth now—zero. She felt ashamed of her relationship with him.

With a determined nod, she vowed in her heart she would have nothing to do with the male half of the world. And she'd explain that to Mike Davis tonight. That would circumvent her father's tricks.

Once the sheriff understood, he'd leave her alone.

She picked him up at seven, having made their reservations for seven-thirty. She figured she could make her explanations during the half hour drive and be able to relax for the rest of the evening.

Ha!

It took five seconds to realize the man affected her senses. Like her father, he also wasn't a man who could be ignored. She was getting tired of those comparisons.

"Evening, Caroline," he said. Dressed in a navy blue suit, a crisp white shirt and a red-and-blue tie, he looked like a powerful CEO.

"I—I didn't dress up." She stumbled over the words, embarrassed.

To her surprise, he leaned over and kissed her cheek. "You look beautiful."

She'd worn navy slacks topped by a winter-white sweater that hugged her hips.

"In fact," Mike said, "I think we match."

She couldn't argue with him, but she didn't want to agree, either. "Mike, we need to talk."

That eyebrow slipped up. She forced her gaze away from his hazel eyes. He tucked his arm under hers and led them to her SUV. "I can drive if you want me to," he offered.

"No, that's all right. I invited you."

He opened her door for her before he circled the vehicle to the passenger side. He waited until she had driven them out of Rawhide before he asked, ''How's Tracey?''

Her mind flew to her patient. That morning, Tracey's parents had arrived from Denver. Beth and Jenny didn't know their grandparents very well, but the girls had stayed out of school and gone with them to pack their belongings.

''Tracey is much better. I'm going to release her in the morning.''

''Good. Because the judge set the bail this morning and I imagine her husband will come up with the money by tomorrow.''

''You can't hold him longer?''

''Not according to the law.''

''Isn't there anything you can do?''

He grinned. ''I'm afraid even sheriffs have to obey the law.''

She couldn't hold back a smile in appreciation of his easygoing attitude, his good nature.

''How do you do it?'' she asked.

''Do what?''

''Stay so relaxed.''

He gave her a serious look. ''I learned a long time ago that the best I can do is control myself. Everyone else is in charge of their lives. I can only do so much. I've heard that's a difficult concept for doctors.''

''Yes, it is,'' she admitted. ''After you save a life, you begin to think you have the power of life. But you do learn you have limitations after you lose a patient for no explicable reason.''

''That must be tough.''

The sympathy in his voice brought tears to her eyes. What was wrong with her? She'd given up crying after her two rotations in the ER. She cleared her throat. "Yes, it is. But I guess it keeps you humble."

"A lawman deals with the same thing when he fails to resolve a situation except by using his weapon."

She'd never thought of Mike's job from that perspective. "Surely all lawmen don't feel that way."

"Maybe not. But I don't think they're doing a good job if that's their only response."

"How did you come to that conclusion?"

"Uncle Bill. He spent some time with me when I was a boy. He knew how easy it was to impress me with his gun. He made sure I understood how to handle it."

"I didn't realize you knew Sheriff Metzger that well."

"After I grew up, we didn't spend that much time together, but we talked frequently."

"Have you talked to him since he went to Arizona?"

"Sure. He's very protective of Rawhide and its people," Mike said with a laugh.

"I've wondered if having to shoot Patience's brother-in-law contributed to his decision to retire."

Mike didn't answer at once. Then he said, "Maybe. But the man gave him no choice. If he'd managed to get his gun again, he would've taken more shots at Patience and Jim. Bill had no other option."

"I know. Dad told me. And we're all grateful for Sheriff Metzger's courage. That man was insane."

"Yeah. The mind is a powerful thing."

"Yes. At one time I thought I'd become a psychiatrist, but my interests changed."

"Why?"

"For a couple of reasons. There would've been no place for me here in Rawhide, for one. My pediatric specialty allowed me to fit right in to Jon's family practice clinic. And it turns out I like family practice."

Before she could go on, he asked, "I thought you didn't want to come back?"

She regretted becoming so involved in the conversation. Now what could she say? And what about explaining the situation to him? She'd thought that would be easy to do. Instead she hadn't even broached the subject and they were already in Buffalo.

"Um, I thought…" She stopped, not sure what to say, then finally murmured, "I don't know."

She parked her SUV in the lot at the French restaurant. Judging from the cars, Le Mouton Bleu was the place to be. "The blue sheep?" she asked.

"That's the place."

"And ranchers eat here?"

"Your dad recommended it."

Mike escorted her into the restaurant. A huge fireplace dominated the scene, burning brightly. Tables were spaced around it at discreet distances from each other, allowing privacy. All the tables were covered with blue linens. In the center of each table was a darker blue vase filled with pale blue columbines.

"How charming," Caroline exclaimed.

"So I've been told."

"By my father?"

"I do talk to other people, Caroline," Mike said with a smile. "Ben Afton brought his wife here because he'd made her mad. He wanted to apologize. He said it worked like a charm."

Caroline frowned. "I don't need to apologize to you."

"Is that the only reason someone would come here?"

"Good evening, *monsieur et madame*," the maître d' said, interrupting their discussion. "Your name?"

"Caroline Randall," she said calmly.

"Ah, yes, Dr. Randall. Right this way, please."

Mike grinned. "Another person you gave your title to."

"No," she whispered as she followed the man. "My nurse made the reservation for me."

Once they were seated, a waiter immediately appeared at the table to point out the specials.

They both listened to him without comment. Caroline tried to keep a pleasant look on her face when the young man mispronounced his way through the menu. Mike told him they'd like a few minutes to consider the choices.

Caroline dipped her chin behind the menu. "Thank you," she whispered after the waiter had gone.

"No problem. You maintained a stiff upper lip during that massacre of the French language. I was afraid I wouldn't be able to last as long."

"You speak French?" she asked, shock in her voice.

His eyes narrowed, and he leaned back in his chair. "Some. Enough to recognize a Frenchman would commit suicide after that recitation."

"I didn't mean to be insulting, Mike. But we're a long way from Gay Paree. You surprised me."

"I would think a doctor would know better than to take everything at face value," he said softly. "You'd better make your decision, Caroline. Our waiter is approaching."

She nodded and looked at her menu. When the young man stopped by her chair, she said, "I'll have the roast beef and vegetables."

"I'll have the same," Mike said smoothly, handing him his menu.

With a look of relief, the waiter hurried away.

"I wonder if he has to catch the snails if we order them," Mike said in amusement, as if he didn't think she'd insulted him. "The relief on his face that we ordered the roast beef indicated he'd just avoided something unpleasant."

Caroline laughed. "So tell me, how do you know French?"

"I lived next to a Frenchwoman. She was having trouble making a living and I asked her to give me French lessons."

"So that's why you wanted to come here? Because you can speak French?"

"No. Any French restaurant that requires its patrons to speak French had better not be located in Wyoming."

They smiled and nodded in unison. Mike really was a charming dinner companion. A charming man, she corrected herself. Every moment with him could be enjoyable. But—

"Mike, we need to talk," she repeated abruptly.

She decided if she didn't speak now, he'd change the subject and she'd forget what had to be said.

"Over dinner?"

"No, now. I...it's awkward, so I guess I'll just blurt it out. My father is known for his matchmaking. He managed to get all three of his brothers married. As the Randall family has expanded, he's taken credit for all the marriages. And you're in his sights."

Her dramatic finish didn't affect Mike's expression in the slightest. He took a sip of the iced tea he'd ordered. "I see."

"No, I don't think you do. That's why you were invited to dinner yesterday, and it's the reason I was seated beside you. I'm the one you're supposed to marry."

Again there was no response, except for a half smile crossing his lips. "Really?"

After a moment of staring at him, she said, "You figured it out, didn't you?"

"Your father isn't known for his subtlety."

"Then why did you accept the invitation?"

"I heard Red's cooking is something special. You won't find many lawmen who turn down a free meal, much less one like Red cooked." His smile widened.

"You're playing a dangerous game, Mike Davis. My father may not be subtle, but he's also not weak."

"I know."

"Then—"

"I'm counting on you being stronger than him."

"I am. That is, I intend to be. I'm not going to marry, but—"

"Why?"

"I don't have to give a reason!" she snapped.

"Okay."

"Why aren't you upset?"

"Caroline, we came for a nice meal because you felt bad about how you behaved when you first arrived. Let's just enjoy the evening."

She couldn't believe her ears. He acted as if there was no problem. She started to warn him again, when he nodded toward a couple walking outside the restaurant.

"I know that guy but I can't place the name. Eric…"

She followed Mike's eyes and saw the man and woman through the window as they stepped into the pool of light from the streetlamp. "Yes, he's Eric Williams. He works on my uncle Griff's ranch."

"Do you know the woman he's with?"

"No, but I thought he was engaged to Holly Gambil. I guess they broke up," Caroline said slowly, trying to remember if she'd heard anything about that relationship.

The nervous waiter brought their salads.

Just as Caroline was about to begin her meal, a blur of movement outside made her look up.

"There's Holly now," she said, indicating a woman who'd stepped out of the shadows against the building. Then Caroline rushed to get out the words. "Mike, she has a gun!"

Even as she spoke, Mike leaped from his chair and rushed outside to the young woman. But he was too late to save Eric Williams. Holly had fired the gun from point-blank range. But she wasn't finished. She turned to his companion and raised the weapon to fire again. By that time Mike had reached her and knocked the gun from her hand. It went off, but instead of her heart, the bullet struck the young woman's shoulder.

Caroline grabbed her keys and thrust them at a nearby waiter. "I'm a doctor. My bag is in the gray SUV parked in the first row. Unlock it and get my bag. Hurry."

The shocked waiter ran out the back door, and Caroline went out to the woman on the ground. Blood flowed from the wound in her shoulder and she collapsed into unconsciousness.

"I'm a doctor," Caroline announced again, and the few people who'd run out backed away. "Get me some clean napkins," she ordered as she began staunching the blood.

In the meantime, Mike had disarmed Holly and told the maître d' to call the local police, along with an ambulance. Chaos began to dissipate as Caroline worked on her patient and Mike held the shooter still. Holly was sobbing and babbling, but her words made no sense.

When the police arrived, Mike turned her over with a brief description of what had happened. He handed the gun over, as well. "We think it's a crime of passion. She was engaged to this man. Both of them are from Rawhide."

"And the wounded one?"

"We don't know her."

He'd shown them his badge, and after the first policeman put Holly in handcuffs and led her away, the other one, obviously the senior of the two, asked, "You new to Rawhide? What happened to Bill Metzger?"

"He retired."

"Oh. I hadn't heard. Did he—"

"Excuse me," Mike interrupted. "I want to check on the doc." He stepped to Caroline's side and squatted down. "You doing all right?"

"I'm all right. But I'm not so sure about her." She looked at the two ambulance drivers.

"I'll ride with you guys. Mike, can you follow with my car?"

"Sure, honey. Will you be all right?"

She looked surprised at his question. "Of course."

"I assume Eric is dead?"

"Yes."

Mike stood and then helped Caroline to her feet as the two men put the woman on the stretcher. Caroline immediately pressed the wound, stopping the flow, which had resumed. She walked alongside the stretcher.

Mike was about to follow when a waiter handed him a set of keys. "These are the lady doctor's."

"Oh, yes, thank you."

Their own waiter was standing there, ringing his hands. "But what about your dinner? The roast beef is ready."

Mike stared at him. "Tell you what. Put it in some to-go boxes and I'll take it with me."

Relieved, the waiter hurried away. The maître d' told him to add two desserts. Then he announced to all the diners that everyone was entitled to free desserts. After all, they'd be detained there for a while so the cops could question any potential witnesses.

Mike reached for his wallet to pay for the dinner, but the maître d' stopped him.

"*Monsieur,* you owe nothing. Thank you for ending the distress at once. You and your lady were very helpful. Your dinner is on the house."

"That's not necessary," he protested.

"Please, *monsieur.* It is my pleasure. We hope you will try us again on a quieter night."

Mike put away his money. To insist would hurt the man's pride. "Thanks, we will."

They shook hands just as the waiter came out with several large sacks. "Could you carry them to the car for me? I think my hands may be dirty."

"Of course, sir."

That way Mike could reward him out of sight of his boss.

When he reached the hospital, he found Caroline in the ER, talking to another doctor, Mike assumed, judging by the scrubs the man was wearing. A surge of jealousy struck him and he fought it down before he reached them.

"Oh, Mike, you're here. This is Dr. George Kenny."

Mike took his hand in a firm shake.

"Mike is the sheriff in Rawhide. He disarmed the shooter and prevented anyone else from being injured."

"Good thing you were there, Sheriff. You and Caroline. She saved that young woman's life."

"Yes, she did. Is there anything else to be done, Doctor? Our night's been rather eventful, and we're both tired."

"Of course. No, we have everything under control."

After they shook hands again, Mike led Caroline out to the SUV. "Want me to drive?"

She'd been determined to be independent. But the night's events seemed to make such rules silly. "That would be wonderful."

He helped her in and then circled the truck to get behind the wheel. "Do you smell our dinner? It's on the back seat."

Caroline looked over her shoulder, surprised. "I smelled roast beef, but I thought I was imagining it."

"I thought maybe we could eat once we finish up with the repercussions of tonight."

"We have to tell Holly's parents she's been arrested?"

"I told the policeman we'd do that. It will come easier from us than it would from a stranger on the phone. And you said Eric worked for your uncle?"

"Yes. I'll call him now before they go to bed." She pulled out a cell phone as Mike drove, listening to her end of the conversation.

"Uncle Griff? It's Caroline." She gave him all the details of the night's events. "No, I don't know the woman's name," she replied to Griff's question.

"We went through her purse," Mike said. "It's Serena Samuels. She lives in Buffalo."

Caroline repeated the information. "No, we're going to Holly's parents' home now to tell them in person." She looked at Mike with a question in her eyes, and he nodded.

"Yes, it will be easier for them. Thanks, Uncle Griff."

Mike glanced at her quickly. "Is your uncle going to notify Eric's next of kin?"

"Yes. He says he has the information on file. He thinks Eric's from a little town in southern Colorado." She sat there, staring straight ahead. "He's always played around. When he hooked up with Holly, several people warned him not to break her heart. But I guess he did, anyway."

"I guess so. People don't change just because other people tell them to."

"No."

"We learned something tonight."

"What are you talking about?"

"We have some things in common."

"What's that?"

"We don't stop working when five o'clock comes around. Even if we're not in uniform, we both respond to people in need." He kept his eyes on the road.

"I guess that's true. But you had the dangerous part. She could've shot you."

Mike shrugged it off. "Honey, I'm six foot four, and Holly was five-one or -two and probably a hundred pounds."

"A bullet doesn't care," Caroline said harshly. She'd learned that lesson in Chicago.

"True, but I didn't give her a chance to shoot me."

"I know," Caroline whispered. "I'm glad."

Instead of continuing the conversation, Mike reached out and took her hand. They rode silently into the night.

When they reached Rawhide, Caroline directed him to Holly's parents' house. The Gambils were a quiet couple, liked and respected by their neighbors. Caroline dreaded telling them what their daughter had done.

"Do you want to stay in the car?" Mike asked, as if he'd read her mind.

"I'd love to, but I'm not going to do that." With a sigh, she pulled her hand free from his and got out of the SUV. They walked up the sidewalk and rapped on the door.

Mr. Gambil was considerably older than Caroline's father; in fact, he looked a little frail. His wife was small and quiet. They both stared at Caroline and Mike, surprise on their faces.

"Hello, Sheriff, Caroline," the man said.

"May we come in for a minute, Mr. Gambil?" Mike asked.

"Well, of course. We weren't expecting company, you know, but you're welcome anytime." The man led them into a neat living room.

Mrs. Gambil leaned toward Caroline. "I'm afraid Holly isn't in this evening, but I'll tell her you came by, Caroline. We're all so glad to have you back in town."

Caroline swallowed, trying to think of how to break the news.

"Mrs. Gambil, this isn't a social call," Mike said softly. "I'm afraid your daughter is in trouble."

The older woman's gaze shifted from Mike to Caroline and back again. "Is she all right? Has there been an accident?"

Mr. Gambil turned so pale Caroline thought he was going to pass out.

"No!" Caroline hurriedly said, reaching for Mrs. Gambil's hands. "Holly is fine."

The sobs slowed, but not much.

"Mr. Gambil, your daughter shot and killed Eric Williams this evening, and she was arrested in Buffalo for murder."

Caroline was glad Mike had gotten right to the point. At least they now knew the truth.

Mr. Gambil grabbed his chest and passed out. His wife screamed his name and dropped to his side, putting her arms around him.

"I'll get your bag for you," Mike whispered, and ran back to the car.

Caroline tried to pry Mrs. Gambil's arms from her husband so she could tend to him. When Mike returned, he helped her with the woman.

Caroline pulled out her stethoscope and said, "Call Mom and Jon. We're going to need some help."

Chapter Six

They took Mr. and Mrs. Gambil to the clinic. Because Caroline suspected a heart attack, Jon met them there to help her evaluate the older man's condition. That left Mike with the wife. She was hysterical, first fearing her husband's death. Then she was sure her daughter would be hanged.

Mike tried to calm her, but he had limited success. When Caroline's aunt Anna and B.J. walked in, he felt like a drowning man suddenly finding a boat. Anna, a licensed midwife, helped the nurse give Mrs. Gambil a tranquilizer, while B.J. called Nick Randall.

"Nick, these people need some legal advice. Their daughter has been arrested for murder. I know you don't usually do that kind of law, but…"

She hung up the phone a minute later. "Nick is coming over. He said he could at least get some information and figure out if there is someone in Buffalo who can help."

"I don't know their financial situation," Mike said awkwardly.

"Don't worry about it. Nick funded a grant to provide legal services for anyone in Rawhide. If he can't handle the work, the grant pays for another lawyer to take over."

"That's wonderful, B.J. I was pretty relieved to see you and Anna. Now I know why Caroline told me to call you."

"We all try to pitch in, Mike. That's what family is for." She sat next to him. "Sounds like your dinner didn't go too smoothly." She gave him a sympathetic smile.

"No, it didn't. We never got to eat."

"Oh, you must be hungry. Do you want me to send someone to the café to get you some food?"

"No, thanks. We have our meal in Caroline's SUV. When she's finished, we'll heat it up and eat together."

"If it's still in the car, it may be frozen by now. It's pretty cold out there."

"How long do you think they'll be?" Mike asked with a sigh.

B.J. turned to Anna, who was sitting with a now calm Mrs. Gambil. "What do you think?"

"If you'll keep an eye on Mrs. Gambil, I'll go see how things are going." With a nod, Anna left the waiting room.

Mike sighed again. "Nice to have someone who can go through those doors and get answers."

B.J. laughed. "Yes, it is." She heard the clinic door open and close and said, "That will either be Nick or Jake. I left word for him to come, too," she said.

It was Nick who walked into the waiting area. Mike had met him once, but he'd been dressed in a suit and tie. Now he looked like anyone in Rawhide, wearing jeans, boots, a cowboy hat and a sheepskin coat.

"Evening, B.J., Mrs. Gambil, Sheriff," he said, nodding to them. "Mrs. Gambil, can I talk to you for a few minutes?"

B.J. and Mike looked at each other, then he spoke up. "Mrs. Gambil was given a sedative. She might not be able to tell you much. But I can explain what happened."

"Thanks, Sheriff. I appreciate that."

"Make it Mike," he said as he stood up, extending his hand.

B.J. directed them to the adjacent doorway. "In there you'll find a place to sit and a pot of hot coffee."

Mike released a breath of relief and followed Nick into a small meeting room. The lawyer sat at a round table and took out a legal pad and pen from his briefcase.

Mike got them coffee and straddled a chair, blowing into the steaming brew. "I don't think this will take long. It was pretty simple for all its devastation."

"What happened?"

Mike went through the event, expanding on things when Nick asked for clarification. "When it was over, she sobbed hysterically, just like her mother. I'm not sure she'll even remember what she's done."

Nick rubbed his forehead. "What a mess. That boy two-timed everyone. Holly was warned, but she was in love." He gave a disgusted look.

"You don't believe in love?"

Nick smiled wryly. "Don't be silly. I'm one of

those Randalls who fell like a ton of bricks. I adore my wife and child. But she also loves me. It takes two people to find happiness. I'm afraid Eric—God rest his soul—was only out for sex. I wonder if Holly is pregnant."

"I wouldn't know," Mike replied. "Caroline didn't say anything."

"She may not know, either. You know they've got those pregnancy tests that tell the woman without her seeing a doctor. My wife told me the news two weeks before she went to see Jon."

"You've got more experience there than I do."

"So you and Caroline were dining together at that French restaurant?"

Mike gave him a straight look. "And?"

"It doesn't sound like a dull dinner."

Mike grinned. "No, but I'm not sure dinner with Caroline could ever be dull."

"Right. Randall women are bright and beautiful. Hard to resist."

"Especially if you don't try," Mike admitted. "But Caroline seems determined not to marry."

There was a question implicit in Mike's voice, and Nick shrugged his shoulders. "I haven't heard anything, though my wife said something was going on about her return."

"Yeah," Mike said with a sigh. He hadn't intended to let anyone know of his interest in Caroline. He'd already decided he wasn't good enough for her, but if her father thought he was, Mike wasn't going to fight it.

As if thinking of him made him appear, Jake strode into the room. "Glad you could come, Nick. This is terrible business,'' he said, shaking Nick's hand, then Mike's. ''Mike, glad you were able to take care of things…and Caroline.''

''Caroline didn't need anyone to save her. She sprang into action at once. She's a good doctor.''

''Well, of course. But you had to disarm the shooter first. I appreciate it.''

''You're welcome,'' Mike finally said. ''Did B.J. find out how things are going?''

''She said something about you getting your dinner soon. Haven't you eaten yet?''

''No. We brought our meal home from the restaurant. I thought I'd wait until Caroline could join me.''

''Good guy. I bet you're starving.'' Jake was almost rubbing his hands in glee.

''It wouldn't be the first meal I've missed in life, Jake. It's not that big a deal,'' Mike said, feeling uncomfortable.

B.J. opened the door. ''They're cleaning up now, Mike. Caroline is getting ready to go.''

''Thanks.'' He stood up, suddenly very eager to leave the clinic. He didn't want to say anything to encourage Jake, and he was afraid he might if he spent much more time there. He walked back to the waiting room, followed by Jake and Nick.

''Where is Mrs. Gambil going for the night?'' Mike asked B.J. ''I don't think she can go home by herself.''

''No, of course not,'' B.J. assured him. ''They'll give her a bed here. She'll want to stay with her husband, and Caroline wants the nurse to keep an eye on her, too.''

''Good.'' He might've said more, but Caroline

came in and drew all his attention. She looked tired, but still beautiful. Jake hugged her, and Mike wished he himself had that right.

"How's Mr. Gambil?" he asked.

Caroline let out a relieved sigh. "He's doing well, resting comfortably. It doesn't look like a heart attack, as I first feared. Probably it was just anxiety, though he gave us a scare."

Mike approached her. "Ready for dinner?" he asked with a smile.

Caroline gave him a tired smile. "I think I'll pass on eating. I just want to fall into bed."

He stepped closer. "I waited for you. Just eat a little before you go to bed."

With another sigh, she said, "Okay, just a little."

Mike risked a glance at Jake, who'd remained strangely silent. He saw B.J.'s boot on top of her husband's, obviously restraining him from prompting his daughter. Mike nodded to Caroline's mom in gratitude, and she smiled in reply.

"Good night, everyone," he called as he urged Caroline to the door. He was never so grateful for the cold night air.

STRIDING OVER TO JAKE, Nick patted him on the back. "Neatly done, Jake. And I'm proud of you for not saying anything."

"Yeah, me, too," the older man said, glaring at his wife.

Nick grinned. "Well, Mike seems like a nice man."

"He is, and fast-acting, too." Jake nodded to himself. "I'm right on track."

"This is none of your business, Jake Randall," B.J. said. "You leave Caroline alone. She has to find her own happiness."

Instead of arguing with his wife, Jake wrapped his arm around her and led her toward the door. "I just hope she's as lucky as I was."

MIKE DROVE the short distance to Caroline's house while she sat slumped against the door, her eyes closed. When he'd parked the truck, he reached over and touched her cheek. "We're home, honey. Go in and grab a shower while I heat up dinner."

"I don't—"

"Don't bother dressing again. Just put on a robe. You've got ten minutes."

Somehow, it didn't seem worth arguing. Maybe because the thought of a hot shower was too tempting. Afterward, she wrapped herself in a long robe that zipped up from her toes to her neck, and pulled on woolen socks. She combed her hair back and re-entered the living room.

Mike had built a fire in the fireplace and had two plates full of roast beef and vegetables set out on the coffee table. There was a loaf of French bread on a separate plate.

"They sent the bread, too?" she asked, smiling.

"I think the maître d' would've given us just about anything. We have dessert, too."

The food looked delicious, the setting warm and inviting. Giving in to the moment, she sank onto the couch in front of the fire, and, side by side, they slowly ate their late dinner.

Caroline leaned back after. She'd consumed about half her roast beef. "Oh, I can't eat another bite!"

"You can save that for lunch tomorrow, but you've got to taste the dessert." He got up to retrieve a white pastry and she felt a sudden chill. Sitting close to Mike had felt so cozy, so warm. Even intimate, when their arms touched or their legs brushed.

In front of her, Mike opened the box to reveal tiny masterpieces. "We have *pain au chocolat* and Napoleons. Which would you prefer?"

Caroline licked her lips in anticipation. "I think I'll have a Napoleon now and maybe the *pain au chocolat* for breakfast."

. "Good idea." He slipped the pastry on a plate for her and one for himself. Then he slid back onto the sofa.

"Good thing you were there tonight," he said, leaning back against the cushions. Since he'd had his arm on the back of the sofa, it fell to her shoulders.

His touch felt right, good, after their long night together. "I think we were both pretty useful tonight." She relaxed and lay her head on his shoulder. "I've been thinking about what you said."

"What was that?"

"About our jobs having similarities. In Chicago, I only dated other doctors because they understood when I'd had a hard day or had to cancel at the last minute."

"Sounds kind of boring," he said. Then he kissed her temple.

At least she thought he did. The touch had been so light, she wasn't sure. She'd feel like a fool if she reprimanded him. Besides, he felt good, solid. "Oh, I suppose so."

"So there's no one special in Chicago?"

She gave him a sharp look. "Why do you think that?"

"Because either there is no one or your father doesn't like him. Otherwise he wouldn't be match-making."

Caroline jerked her head from Mike's shoulder and sat up. "My personal life is none of your business."

"Are you sure?"

She stared at him, her mouth falling open. "What do you mean?"

"If your father is going to try to matchmake, it seems to involve me, too."

Caroline turned away, arrogance no longer stiffening her shoulders. "I'm sorry," she said softly. "I'll tell him no. I mean, I'll tell him you won't do. I'll make sure he believes me."

"But I think I would do." Mike pulled her gently back against him again and lifted her chin. "I've been wanting to kiss you all night." Then he lowered his head and did so.

Ever since their first encounter—right here in this house—she'd known she was attracted to him. Her gaze frequently focused on his lips, her thoughts frequently wandered to his body. No matter how she warned herself, she couldn't stop wondering what it would be like to spend the night with Mike, to share his bed. When he kissed her, his power over her was obvious. Incredible. Overwhelming. Her arms went around his neck and she pressed against him. This kiss was everything she'd hoped for.

But when he pulled her onto his lap, she realized it was time for her to call a halt before she completely lost her head. "Mike, we—we need to stop. I'm not going to get married."

Somehow, she expected to be thrown on the floor, as if she were damaged goods. That was how she felt. Had felt for four years. Instead, he pulled her closer.

"I don't remember proposing," he whispered, as he trailed kisses down her neck. "But a little loving might persuade me."

He kissed her again, more deeply.

"I—I'm not trying to persuade you, Mike. I—I can't marry." She was having trouble breathing as he ran his hands over her.

"Okay. We won't marry tonight. But we could love each other tonight. We could explore the possibilities of love. We could comfort each other." He unzipped her robe several inches. "I could touch your silken skin. I could feel you pressed against me as I've been imagining all evening."

She knew she should say no, but she couldn't think why at the moment. She felt so good when he touched her.

He lowered the zipper a bit more and kissed the exposed skin. She suddenly found herself removing his tie, unbuttoning his shirt, running her hands over his broad chest.

When he stood, she thought he was leaving her, and she was sure she was going to burst into tears.

"Let's go to bed, Caro. I want to make this a night to remember."

She didn't answer except to gaze up at him. But it was all the answer he needed. In one fluid motion he bent and picked her up in his arms, cradling her against him as he strode purposefully to her bedroom.

Caroline was a tall woman, a capable woman. It wasn't often that a man made her feel small, protected. But Mike made her feel these and many other things she'd never felt before.

When they reached her bedroom, he stood her on her feet and reached for the zipper on her robe. He paused, waiting for her signal before he pulled it down. Then he looked at her sharply. "Are you protected, Caro? I don't have a condom with me."

"Yes, I'm protected," she murmured, reaching for him.

He lay her on the bed and raked her with his gaze. From her flushed cheeks to her creamy breasts and on to her womanhood, his eyes feasted on her. Caroline thought she'd be shocked by his blatant delight, shocked by her own carnal response, but somehow it felt so right, so exciting, so…perfect to be here like this with Mike.

Emboldened, she stood, reached out and undressed him. When they had discarded their bothersome clothes and were skin to skin, sharing the same bed and the same air, she clung to him, warmed by the magic he made her feel.

He fondled her breasts and her nipples hardened. For every one of his actions, she had a reaction—surprising her, arousing her more than Don ever had. Mike reached down between their bodies to touch her center and she felt as if she'd explode from one simple caress of his hand. But his finger was nothing compared to what she felt when he entered her fully.

This was right, she thought. It couldn't feel so good if it weren't.

Mike kissed her and murmured her name against her lips. Then he grasped her bottom and surged into her one more time, and they reached the peak of physical pleasure together.

Caroline fell back onto the bed, closing her eyes, and surrendered to sated exhaustion. Next to Mike's warm body, with his arm pressed to her middle and holding her close, she drifted off to sleep, a smile on her lips. It was the perfect end to the day.

MIKE ENVISIONED WAKENING to a morning kiss, a little conversation, maybe even a repeat of loving. Somehow the morning didn't quite play out that way.

He woke to a shriek, and the sight of Caroline jumping out of bed, running to the shower. Obviously neither of them had responded to the alarm. He couldn't vouch for her, but he knew he'd never overslept…until now.

Caroline was halfway to the shower when she seemed to realize she was naked and he was in her bed.

"Oh!" She searched for cover and came up with her robe from the floor. "Mike, I can't—we mustn't—we need to forget what happened last night. And you need to go home. You can get dressed while I'm in the shower." She backed into the bathroom and closed the door.

Mike lay in her bed, staring at the door, trying to adjust from expectations to reality. She wanted him out. Why? Last night had been wonderful.

He got up and pulled on his clothes, checking the

clock. Nine. He should've been on duty an hour ago. Now he had to skulk home in his rumpled suit and slip upstairs for a quick shower and a change of clothes.

Not to mention breakfast.

He waited until Caroline opened the bathroom door, this time wrapped in a towel. At her look of alarm, he raised his hands. "I'm leaving, but we're going to talk about this, Caroline. It's not something I'm about to forget." Then he left her house.

Caroline stood there, frozen. He'd looked good, even though his suit was wrinkled. He was a sensual man. And last night had been incredible. That was why they had to forget it. Thank goodness he'd gone.

She found clean clothes, grateful that Jon had established the practice of casual clothes for the doctor on duty. A lab coat made for great camouflage. With her hair still wet, she braided it and headed for the front door. Then she remembered the *pain au chocolat* she'd saved for breakfast.

When she opened the box, she found two pieces of pastry, which meant Mike hadn't taken his. With a guilty grin, she grabbed the box to take with her. They'd have coffee made at the clinic, and she was going to enjoy the pastries—both of them.

Patients didn't start coming until ten o'clock, so she had a little time. Jon would've looked in on Mr. Gambil for her when the nurses told him she hadn't come in, so she slipped into her office without seeing anyone. After she hung up her coat and put on the lab coat, she found Connie, one of the daytime nurses, and checked in with her before grabbing a cup of coffee.

"So you made it?" Jon asked from behind her.

"Sorry." She turned around but couldn't stop the blush that instantly warmed her cheeks. "I was so tired I slept through my alarm. I couldn't believe it when I woke up at nine."

"No problem. Since I had yesterday off for the first time in years, I won't begrudge you sleeping in after a late night." His tone was sincere but she couldn't help noticing his curious smile.

"I won't let it happen again," she hurriedly said.

"Hey, Caro, we're partners. I'm not your supervisor."

"I know, but I feel bad about—"

"That's the nice thing about a private practice. We get to make the rules." He followed her into her office, pulled out a chair and sat. "Now, let me fill you in. I looked in on Mr. Gambil. He had a good night. Nick stopped by a few minutes ago and picked up Mrs. Gambil to go with him and see about bailing Holly out of jail."

"Will he be able to? She did murder Eric."

"I know, but Nick's going to try. By the way, what do you think about our new sheriff?"

The abrupt change of topic unsettled her, as did the topic itself. Why was he asking her about Mike? "Excuse me?" she murmured.

"Well, you two did have quite an exciting evening. I just wonder what you make of him."

She took a bite of pastry and then sipped some coffee before she answered. "He seems to know his job well."

Jon's big smile acknowledged her cautious answer. "Yeah. I like him, too."

"Jon, don't start. Dad is going to have to work on Josh or one of the other single Randalls. I'm not on the marriage block."

"Why not? Now that there are two of us, we should be able to manage a personal life, too. Even by myself, I did all right."

"I agree. You did fine. But that has nothing to do with me. I worked hard to get where I am and I intend to have a great career and take care of my patients."

"All work and no play—" Jon began.

"Out!" She waved an arm toward the door. "I'm having my breakfast in peace."

"Yes, ma'am. I'll talk to you later." With a mock salute he headed down the hall to his own office.

Caroline sank into the chair behind her desk and chewed on the slightly stale pastry. It still tasted good. And she still felt guilty for taking Mike's share. But life wasn't always fair.

Otherwise, she wouldn't have to give up Mike Davis.

Chapter Seven

Mike took an early lunch to make up for missing breakfast. He wanted to pick up two sandwiches and go to the clinic, but he didn't dare do that until he'd talked to Caroline and straightened things out.

He didn't know what her problem was, but he wanted it cleared up right away. He wanted to share Caroline's bed tonight—and every night. Damn, he thought with a smile, the woman was addictive.

Throughout the day, she stayed on his mind. Several times his men teased him about the smile he displayed.

"You'd think all the bad guys were locked up, the way you're smiling," Harry said, a question in his gaze.

"Compared to Chicago, boys, this job is a vacation," he assured them, hoping his answer would remove any suspicion about him and Caroline.

Truth was, he wasn't thinking about the bad guys—any guys, for that matter. Caroline left no room in his mind for anyone else.

Since he'd awakened in her bed, he couldn't stop thinking about how she'd responded to his touch, how her body had seemed to come alive under his. They'd been great together. So why had she been so skittish this morning? He'd have chalked it up to morning-after jitters had it not been for her comments. *We need to forget what happened last night...* As if he could. *I can't marry...*

Not "I *don't want* to marry," but "I *can't* marry." As a lawman, Mike was attuned to the words people chose when he questioned them. Like many people with something to hide, Caroline's word choice was peculiar.

He'd wanted to talk to her about her marriage phobia this morning, find out what she meant. Surely she wasn't frigid, or scared of sex. Did she think she couldn't devote the time to her career, maybe?

Why does it matter so much? asked a shrewd inner voice.

Why did it? Mike thought. Because marriage to Caroline had an enticing appeal? Because he worried about her happiness? He shrugged off the questions; the reason didn't really matter. It wasn't as if *he* was going to marry her!

He supposed he should dissuade Jake Randall from his none-too-subtle matchmaking. Caroline was obviously uncomfortable with it. Mike saw pleasant, harmless fun, especially at their Sunday dinner, when she'd come to his aid against that obnoxious Alex Olsen. Her protection of him as a Randall guest tickled him. In Mike's life not many people had ever rushed to his defense, much less a woman.

"There he goes again," another deputy pointed out. "Could this preoccupation have anything to do with Dr. Randall?"

"More likely it has to do with the chocolate cake I had after lunch. Of course, I'm going to have to work it off. Which reminds me, we need to set up a workout schedule."

"You're going to *force* us to work out?" asked Willie Marin, outrage in his voice. At fifty, he was the oldest deputy.

"Yeah, and pay you to do it."

Silence fell as the men stared at him, frowning.

Harry sat up straighter. "You're going to pay us to work out?"

"That's only fair if it's required, isn't it? I'll need to hire at least one other man, but I think we can pay for at least an hour of exercise every day."

"But there's no gym in Rawhide," Willie pointed out. "And I'm not driving to Buffalo to pump iron."

Mike picked up a pen and looked at the man. "So is that an official refusal to cooperate with your superior?" He hadn't challenged much his first couple of weeks on the job, but it was time to let everyone know who was in charge.

"Uh, no, I mean…" Fear was on the man's face, and Mike was satisfied.

"What I was going to suggest," he said calmly, as if he hadn't been challenged, "is to clean out that storeroom in the back. I've got a few pieces of equipment and I think I could raise the money for the cost of several more. After all, Rawhide supports us well."

There was a real shift in attitude at his suggestion. But a couple of men still remained unconvinced.

"Your uncle never suggested anything like this."

Mike smiled. "Uncle Bill was older than all of you." Late fifties, he thought. "He wouldn't require something of you he wasn't willing to do. But if I'm going to trust my life to any of you, I want you in good shape. You should feel the same way.''

"He's got a point," Harry replied.

"I'd think target practice is more important than working on a treadmill or lifting weights," Willie grumbled.

Mike smiled even more broadly. They were feeding him the perfect comments. "That brings me to something else I want to talk about. I don't want guns used unless it is absolutely a question of life or death. Talk is the first weapon. Brute strength is second. Gunfire is your last option.''

"Are you saying Bill shouldn't have shot Peters?" Willie asked in outrage. Of all the deputies, he'd been the closest to Bill Metzger.

"No, I'm not. That was the only possible response Bill had to ensure the safety of the innocent.''

Willie nodded in agreement, but he still had a disgruntled look on his face.

"So, it will take a little while to get the back room organized, but I'd like everyone to report to work in warm-ups and jog the first hour of duty. If you can't jog that long, plan to alternate walking and jogging. You'll be partners, depending on who's working with you. Then you can shower, change and start work.''

Mike began studying the paperwork piled up on his desk to indicate the discussion was closed. For some time now he'd intended to discuss an exercise program and firearm use with his staff, though he hadn't planned it for today. But the discussion allowed him to successfully avoid talk of his love life. That was the important thing.

Now he'd have to make a note to approach some of the local ranchers about his plan right away.

EVERYONE ASSUMED CAROLINE had come in late that morning because of her activities the night before. And they were right, of course, but it was her activity with Mike that had caused her to oversleep, not her activity with Mr. Gambil. She struggled to keep her blushes at a minimum whenever the subject came up.

At lunchtime, she got one of the nurses to go pick up some food from the café. She hadn't had time to fix a lunch that morning, even though that was her usual practice.

Time. That had always been a problem in Chicago. But she hadn't thought it would be a problem in Rawhide, especially as she shared the work with Jon.

Her partner poked his head in her office. "I'm meeting Tori for lunch at the café. Want to join us?"

"I wish I could, but Connie's gone to pick me up a salad."

"So stick it in the fridge for tomorrow."

She hesitated, worrying about running into Mike. But she squared her shoulders and gave an abrupt nod. "Okay."

"You look like you're going to face a firing squad. It's only lunch, Caroline. You okay?"

"I'm fine. Just trying to get used to the routine." She stood, removed her lab coat and grabbed her outer coat. Then she followed Jon to the door. When they passed the nurse's station, she asked the nurse on duty to tell Connie to put the salad in the fridge. "I'll be at lunch with Dr. Wilson and his wife."

"I have my beeper," Jon added. "You can reach either of us that way."

As they walked off, Caroline said, "I guess I need to get one."

"We should've already ordered one for you, but...well, we weren't sure you were going to come. Or stay if you came."

Caroline bit her bottom lip. She hadn't intended to make Jon think that. Unfortunately, it was true.

"I thought I might be bored, that there wouldn't be enough work for both of us." She gave a rueful smile. "I didn't realize how hard you've been working."

Jon smiled in return. "It comes and goes. Some weeks I don't have many patients. Here, when that happens, I cut back my hours and spend time with our son and help out at home. Since Tori's pregnant again, she tires out early. Other weeks I never seem to get caught up."

"In Chicago we never got a respite. I think I might like it here, after all."

He gave her a long look. Then he said, "I'm glad. We finally did order your beeper. It should be here any day."

She was surprised at the relief she felt. And she insisted to herself it had nothing to do with Mike Davis.

At lunch, she asked Tori if anyone had heard from Nick on whether he'd gotten Holly released on bail.

"Yes," Tori said, a hint of a smile on her face.

"Why the smile?" Jon asked.

"Nick said he thought the sheriff there would've

paid him to take her away. She'd been crying nonstop since they'd locked her up.''

"She was like that last night, too," Caroline muttered.

"I think we can go ahead and discharge Mr. Gambil," Jon said. "That'll make for a nice family reunion."

"Great, Jon. I'll drop by after work and check up on him."

"Good. That's the other thing about this job. You have more than a professional relationship with a lot of the patients."

"That doesn't surprise me, since I'm related to half the citizens of Rawhide."

They all laughed, since that statement could describe each of them.

Jon held up his coffee cup. "Here's to our partnership, Caro. I'm glad you've decided to stay."

All three touched their cups together.

WHEN CAROLINE RETURNED to the clinic, she found a message to call her mother. She slipped on her lab coat and sat down behind her desk. She had about fifteen minutes before her first afternoon patient.

"Mom? You called?"

"Yes, dear. I just wanted to make sure you were okay after your ordeal last night."

"It wasn't that bad. When I used to do eighteen-hour shifts in the ER, I made it."

"But Connie said you arrived at work late this morning."

Caroline rolled her eyes. "True, I overslept, but I don't intend to make a habit of it." She'd have to make sure of it if her every move was going to be reported to her mother.

"All right, dear. Want to come to dinner tonight? You could ask Mike to come, too."

"Mom! I didn't expect you to help Dad."

"I just thought Mike might deserve a reward for his performance last night."

Caroline was glad no one was watching her, because the "performance" that came to her mind was not the one her mother meant. "I'm sure he doesn't. Mike is a professional."

"Well, we appreciate him taking such good care of you."

She blushed again. "I'll tell him," she said.

"Oh. So, you'll see him?"

"I would guess so. Rawhide isn't that big a town, Mom."

After a few minutes, B.J. hung up. Caroline reached for her appointment book, and was preparing her patient list when the phone rang again.

"Dr. Randall," she answered.

"Caro, I'm going out to the ranch for dinner. Do you want to come with me?"

She recognized his voice, but she wasn't going to allow Mike Davis to think that. "Who is this?"

"Oh, sorry. It's Mike."

"Why are you going for dinner? Did Mom just call you?"

She could hear puzzlement in his silence. "Actually, Red did. And he suggested I invite you, too. I need to speak with your dad, and—"

"What about?" she interrupted.

"I beg your pardon?"

"I just wondered why you needed to talk to my dad," she hurriedly said.

"It's police business." His voice wasn't as warm as it had been.

"I'm sorry. Mom had just—that is, I'm not going for dinner tonight."

"Then you'd better call Red. I'm not going to upset him. He was real excited to have you there again."

"That's not fair!" she exclaimed. Red was her surrogate grandfather, and she would never disappoint him if she could help it. Was it asking so much, that she let him cook for her? "Fine! I'll go with you. We can talk on the way."

"What will we talk about?"

"Don't play dumb, Mike Davis. You know what we have to talk about!"

"I'll pick you up at six," he said, and hung up the phone.

She wanted to hang up on him, but he'd beaten her to the punch. She squared her jaw. He may have had the last word now, but she'd make sure she got the last word tonight.

"SHERIFF," Willie Martin said, practically meeting him at the door as Mike came in after walking around town.

"Yes, Willie. Did something come up?"

"After lunch I tried to start doing my jogging today, but I had chest pains. I think I need to see the doctor. Is that all right?"

Mike frowned, worrying that he might have asked too much from the fifty-year-old man. "Of course it is. I'll call the clinic. Harry, you go with Willie, okay?''

Mike grabbed his phone and called Jon. He didn't want to talk to Caroline again until he picked her up. ''Dr. Wilson, please. It's Sheriff Davis.'' Then he waited for Jon to come to the phone.

''Anything wrong, Mike?''

''I don't know. I asked my men to start jogging today and Willie is having chest pains. He's on his way over.''

''Hang on,'' Jon said. Mike heard him ordering a room for Willie, alerting his nurse of what was coming. ''Okay, we're ready for him.''

''Thanks, Jon. Bill the office.''

''If all your men are going to start jogging, they should be checked to see what kind of shape they're in. Can the Sheriff's Office afford to do that?''

''Yeah, I guess so.''

''Then have all of them —no, I tell you what. Caro and I will come over tomorrow morning at eight and check the deputies on duty before they go out to run.''

''Are you sure, Jon? I don't want to burden either of you.''

''It won't be a problem. The others can check in here before they go on duty. We'll leave some time in our schedule.''

''Thanks, Jon. You're the best.''

Though Caroline might not think so when she heard what Jon had volunteered her for. Not that it would take that much time. Besides Willie, Mike had only five other deputies on duty during the day, and two night guys.

He sighed, hoping Jon told Caro at once and she

had time to calm down before he picked her up for dinner.

Fifteen minutes later, Harry returned.

"How's Willie?" Mike asked at once, coming out of his office.

"Doc says he's fine. But they're going to keep him overnight to be sure."

"Damn. I should've had him tested before I ordered him to work out."

Harry rubbed the back of his neck. "Boss, don't feel too bad. He didn't do much jogging. He mostly walked."

"You went with him?"

"Yeah," Harry said with a grin. "I jogged in circles waiting for him to catch up. Two blocks and he said he couldn't go on. I'm the one who insisted he keep going, so it's my fault if it's anyone's."

"I gave the order," Mike reminded him. "Anyway, everyone is going to be checked before there's any more jogging."

"We are? Hmm, I hope I get to see Caroline instead of Jon," Harry said with a grin.

Mike tried to keep a calm face, in spite of the jealous pang he felt. "She's too old for you, boy."

"I think that's up to her, boss."

"No harassing, you hear?"

Harry feigned shock. "I'd never do that!"

"Okay. I want you to go over to the general store. They've been losing inventory. Give them some ideas about catching shoplifters, and look for ways they can improve surveillance."

"Yes, sir. Shall I take Steve with me? He worked

there when he was in high school. Might have some insight.''

''Good idea. Check with me when you get back.''

''Yes, sir.''

After the men left, Mike reminded himself how much he liked Harry and how he thought he'd turn out to be one of his best deputies. He shouldn't let his judgment be altered by jealousy.

He drew a deep breath and tried to concentrate on his paperwork. Not on Caroline.

''TOMORROW AT EIGHT? At the Sheriff's Office?''

Jon nodded. ''I thought that would be more efficient. I approve of Mike's intention to keep his men in good shape, but Willie shouldn't have overdone it the first day.''

''Willie jogged for an hour?''

''Well, actually, that's what *he* told me. Harry brought him in, and, privately, he said Willie walked all that time. I think I'll recommend his walking for half an hour and maybe some weight work for fifteen minutes. It ought to improve his health quite a bit.''

''Yes, of course. I noticed the weight he carried. In his present state, he's a heart attack waiting to happen. The rest of them are in pretty good shape, aren't they?''

''I think so, but I'm sure several of them don't do any exercising. Starting can be a shock to the body.''

''Okay. I'll be there at eight in the morning. Will we see everyone?''

''I think we can check the two coming off duty before they leave and then get the two who go on early duty. The others report in at noon. I reckon they'll come over to the office.''

"So we'll see our police jogging all over town now?''

"Harry said Mike is planning on turning the back storeroom into a place to work out. I may offer free exams if he'll let me work out there, too.''

"So I'd be the only bad guy, charging for my work?'' she teased. "I'll just donate mine without demanding anything in return. Then you'll be the bad guy.''

Jon laughed. "Somehow, Caro, I don't think you'll be considered a guy, no matter what.''

"Oh, you!'' She shook her head and went back to work.

Caroline left the clinic at five and, after stopping to check on Mr. Gambil, hurried home. She made her bed when she got there, trying not to recall what had tangled the sheets last night. Then she took a hot shower. It felt so good. Afterward, she dressed in wool slacks and another sweater. She was sure Mike wouldn't be dressed in a suit tonight. Not if he'd told the truth and he was going to her home to do police business.

She wrinkled her nose as she dusted it with powder. She didn't bother with much makeup. Her naturally dark lashes needed no mascara, so she just used a little lipstick and powder.

She checked her watch as she heard a knock on her door. Though Mike was a bit early, she wasn't going to complain. But she'd changed her mind about talking to him on the way out to the ranch. They'd talk on the way home. Then she wouldn't have to spend the evening with him after he was repulsed by her situation.

She opened the door. "Mike, you're early."

"Not much," he assured her. As if it were a natural reaction, his arms slid around her and his lips covered hers in a passionate kiss. She didn't intend to respond. She told herself that even as she did. When he lifted his lips, he buried his face in her hair and drew a deep breath. "I've been waiting for that all day."

"Mike, we can't—I mean, we were going to forget about—"

"Like hell we were. You may be able to, but I can't. I haven't thought of much else all day."

She shoved her way out of his embrace, feeling chilled when she left his warmth. "We'll talk after we have dinner."

"We will?"

"On the way home. Yes, we need to clear the air."

"I like the air just fine." He studied her, making the blood rush to her cheeks.

"I—I need to braid my hair." She hurried from the room, thinking she would leave Mike behind for a few minutes so she could regain her composure.

"Want me to do that for you?"

She spun around. He had followed her. "No. Go sit down. I'll be out in a minute."

He shrugged his shoulders and went back into the living room.

She drew a deep breath. The man was going to drive her crazy. Every time he touched her, she lost control. That had never happened with Don. Another condemnation of their relationship.

After braiding her hair, she gave herself a pep talk

in the mirror. But whatever confidence she'd instilled evaporated the moment she reentered the living room. Just being near Mike made her unsteady.

Best to keep it on a professional level, she told herself. "So I hear you're starting a new physical program for your deputies."

Mike shrugged. "I want them to be in good shape. Makes it less likely they'll resort to gunfire."

The respect she felt for his lawman abilities increased. "I think that's good. I'll be over with Jon in the morning to check out your men."

"I appreciate that. You ready?"

"Yes, of course." She grabbed her coat from the hook by the door.

He took it from her and held it out while she slid her arms in. "Thank you," she said, trying to avoid his touch.

Once they were driving to the ranch, silence reigned. Finally Mike cleared his throat. "You sure you don't want to talk now?"

"I'm sure," she said firmly. "You're going to talk to Dad after dinner?"

"Actually, to Jake and all three of his brothers, and Toby. I understand he has an equal role in decisions on the ranch."

"And Jim, too. He has his own herd, but he also works with the family."

"Oh. Okay."

"So your conversation has nothing to do with me?"

Mike gave her a long look before he turned back to his driving. "Anything I have to say about you will be said to you. At least right now."

"Okay," she said, relief flowing through her. She hadn't quite believed that their dinner tonight had nothing to do with her.

They were warmly greeted when they entered the Randall house. "You're all still acting like I live miles away," Caroline complained. "I'm just in Rawhide now."

Her dad put his arm around her. "We're still glad to see you, honey. And always will be."

She hugged him again. "I'm glad to see you, too."

Jake turned to Mike. "Red said you needed to talk to us?"

Mike shook his extended hand. "Yes, sir. I'm going to make the rounds of all the ranchers to see if they can help out."

"Good. I look forward to hearing what you've got in mind."

The children were gathering around the table, their parents helping them get settled. When Casey saw his basketball coach, he hurried over to shake his hand.

"Coach, I didn't know you'd be here. How are your ribs?"

Mike actually blushed, which amused Caroline. It was good to see him embarrassed for a change.

"They're fine, Casey. I should be back at practice next Monday. How's it going?"

"I tried that move you showed me and it worked like a charm. You should've seen it!"

Pete came and put his hands on his youngest son's shoulders. The high school senior was as tall as his dad. "Casey raves about your help, Mike. We appreciate it."

"My pleasure, Mr. Randall. Casey works hard, which makes it fun to teach him."

Pete beamed. "Make it Pete, Mike. There are too many Randalls."

"All you Randalls better get to the table," Red warned. "And guests, too," he said, looking at Mike. "Or you'll be missing dinner."

"Okay, Red," Casey said. He looked at Mike. "You joining us?"

Pete answered before Mike could. "He's going to eat with us, son. We've got business to take care of."

"Oh. Okay. I'll see you Monday, Coach."

"Okay, Casey."

"Actually," Jake said, coming back to Mike, "we could talk now while the children eat. We usually eat in here after them. Unless you think it will take more time?"

"Not at all. That will be fine." Mike figured it might give him more time alone with Caroline. He'd never complain about that.

Jake said a few words to his brothers and his son, and they all moved into Jake's office.

Mike took one of the chairs offered and waited until everyone was seated. "I won't make this long. I want my staff to maintain a certain physical ability. I've offered to pay them to exercise an hour a day on duty. I believe it lessens the thought of relying on guns to enforce the law. It will require hiring one more deputy, provided we can find someone qualified. And I'd like to turn the storage room at the office into a workout room. I have some equipment and I wondered if maybe the ranchers in the area would be willing to pay for a few other machines."

Jake was frowning, and Mike thought he might not have convinced the Randalls. That would be a problem, since many of the local ranchers would follow their lead.

After a moment of silence, Jake said, "Is that all?"

"I beg your pardon?" Mike replied, not sure what he was asking.

"Is that all you'll need? Money for another deputy and a couple of machines?"

"Well…yes. I realize it's asking a lot, but—"

"I don't think so," Toby answered. "I like your attitude toward violence. When our boys reach the stupid age—or the teenage years, as most people call them—I'd hope they'd get a second chance, instead of being shot."

"That's what I hope, too," Mike said, appreciating his support.

Pete spoke next. "We all like what you're suggesting. We want to be sure you have what you need. Tell us how much money it'll take."

"Well, I hoped…" Mike drew a deep breath. "I was going to ask for donations from all—"

Jake cut him off. "We'll take care of it, Mike, with pleasure. Now, let's go enjoy our meal."

And with that, Mike's pitch was successfully over.

Chapter Eight

Mike wasn't quite sure what the Randalls had agreed to with Jake's promise. Were *they* going to canvass their neighbors for him? He would appreciate it. If he hadn't felt his program was important, he wouldn't have forced himself to approach the ranchers.

Once he and Caroline were back in his SUV, all thought of Jake and money for his deputies' training flew out of Mike's mind. Anytime he was alone with Caroline, she took center stage.

"Did you enjoy dinner?" he asked, hoping to start slowly.

"Yes. Mike, we can't see each other."

She'd just plunged into the deep end.

"So I'm supposed to close my eyes when you go by?" he teased, hoping to lighten the moment.

"You know what I'm talking about. Our…actions got out of hand last night and it mustn't happen again."

"Why?"

"Because nothing could ever come of it."

She was staring straight ahead, never looking at him. He reached out and caught her left hand. She jumped as if he'd struck her, and tried to pull her hand away. "What is it, Caro? We've held hands before."

"But we're not going to do that anymore."

He let her hand go and sped up.

"Why are you going faster?"

"Because I'm not going to have this discussion while I'm driving. It wouldn't look good for the sheriff to veer off the road."

She said nothing, and he concentrated on his driving, determined to get back to her place as soon as possible.

When they reached her house, she didn't open her door. "Wait. We need to talk here. I don't want you to come in."

"That's not very hospitable of you."

"I'm not trying to be hospitable. I'm trying to make my situation clear. And when I get near a bed with you...or a sofa, I forget what I was going to say."

He liked her confusion. It gave him hope that he might be able to talk her into something. "You affect me the same way, sweetheart. Certain men and women strike each other that way."

"I'm not going to marry, Mike. And any liaison between us would ultimately end. I don't want to be hurt."

He sat there, staring at her. "You think I'd dump you? Are you out of your mind?"

"Probably," she agreed with a weary sigh.

"Tell me why you won't marry. Do you think you can't do your job if you're married? I don't see a problem with that. We're both adults. We both function just fine now. Why wouldn't we be able to carry on as married people?''

''You wouldn't want to stay married to me.''

She made that remark with such sad conviction, he stared at her again. Then he reached for her shoulders and swung her around to face him. ''Are you seriously ill?'' he demanded, the agony in his heart echoing in his voice.

''No,'' she whispered.

Now he was getting angry. She'd scared him and he didn't like being scared. ''Tell me right now, Caroline Randall. What are you talking about?''

''I can't have children.''

He frowned and waited for her to continue. Finally, he said, ''Is there more?''

''Isn't that enough?''

''No.'' He didn't elaborate. There was no need to in his mind.

''You say that now. But you'll change your mind. Most men do,'' she assured him. ''I don't want to go through that heartache.''

''Caroline, I'm thirty-five. If having babies was a priority for me, don't you think I would've done something about it earlier?''

''Maybe you haven't met the right woman yet.''

''I've met you.''

''I can't be the right woman for you, Mike. I can't have children!'' She was practically screaming by the time she finished.

''And do I understand this right? If I say I don't care about having children, you think I'm lying?''

''Not lying,'' she said carefully. ''But the day will come when you'll want children.''

"And if I married you, there would be no way to have kids? Adoptions can't be considered? Surrogate motherhood would be impossible? My choice, according to you, would be to dump you for another body?"

She nodded, trying to look away, which was difficult since he still held her shoulders.

"Who did this to you?"

She gave him a sharp look. "What do you mean?"

"What slimeball left you because you can't have children? And how dare you lump me in with him!"

"It wasn't—okay, but I'd been honest and then…his nurse became pregnant. We'd been together for two years and—he had to do the right thing." Caroline was shaking by now, as if it were all her fault.

Mike shook his head. "You come from the Randalls, where every one of the men are stand-up guys, and you fall for some lowlife who treats you like that? And he's stupid, too, if he can use the expression 'doing the right thing' when he obviously has no concept of the right thing!" As if he couldn't stand to be close to her, Mike opened his door and got out into the cold night air. He paced briskly for several minutes, clearly talking to himself. Then he turned and rounded the truck to open her door.

"Get out, Caroline."

She did so, and stood there, waiting for what he would say next.

"I don't know what to call our brief relationship. I know I'm very attracted to you. I know I like you. And I'll be damned if I'll let you compare me to this stupid man of your past. You need to get over him, and stop thinking you have nothing to offer a man. When you do, give me a call! If I'm still available.''

Without another word, he rounded the truck, got behind the wheel and drove off into the night.

CAROLINE HAD NO difficulty awakening early the next morning to meet Jon at the Sheriff's Office. In fact, she was relieved to crawl from the torture chamber formerly called her bed. She'd tossed and turned all night long, Mike's words playing in her mind.

She was over Don; that much she knew. But she'd accepted his behavior as condemnation of her womanhood. And she'd made Mike mad because of it. Was he right? Did life hold the possibility of a happy marriage even though she couldn't have children?

She'd always known about the options of adoption or surrogate motherhood. But she'd felt she would be offering something second best. Randalls always went first class! Her mind was in a jumble, and facing the man who'd made her so crazy wasn't exactly number one on her list of fun things to do.

When she was ready to go, she called Jon to see if he'd left home yet. She didn't want to turn up at the Sheriff's Office alone.

Jon was just about to leave.

''I'm going to stop by the clinic and pick up a scale we're not using,'' he told her. ''I think they'll need one. Then I'll be there.''

''Okay. I'll see you in about five minutes.''

''Right.''

She bundled up for the cold weather and waited another four minutes. She was sure Jon would be there now. Walking briskly to keep warm, she went to the Sheriff's Office.

When she opened the door and realized her partner wasn't there yet, she tried to back out, but Mike had come out of his office and greeted her.

"Morning, Caroline."

"Good morning, Sheriff. Jon isn't here yet?"

"No, but I'm sure he'll arrive soon. Care for a cup of coffee?"

"Yes, thanks." Maybe coffee would help her think more sharply. She needed something.

"Close the door," he reminded her as he walked to the back where they kept the coffeepot.

She closed the door and started after him. Several of the deputies were standing around and she greeted them, relieved to see them there. At least she wasn't alone with Mike.

When the door opened behind her, she assumed it was Jon and turned to greet him. Only Nick and Gabe Randall walked in.

She still didn't know how to tell her twin cousins apart. She smiled. "Nick, Gabe, what are you doing here?"

Before they could answer, Mike put a mug of coffee in Caroline's hand and greeted the two men.

"You don't know which one of us is which, do you?" one of them asked.

Mike grinned. "Seeing the two of you together, frankly, I don't. I hope you're going to give me a hint so I don't make a fool of myself."

"I'm Gabe," one of them said. "I look older because my wife and I have twins. They age you quickly.'' He immediately pulled out pictures of two babies about eighteen months old.

Nick pulled out a picture, too. His baby boy was about nine months old. ''Mine is catching up fast,'' he assured them.

Caroline couldn't help looking at Mike as he admired the pictures. He glanced up and caught her stare. ''Congratulations, guys. Those are good-looking babies.'' He handed back the pictures. ''But it still doesn't tell me why you're here.''

''We're meeting Jake and the crew here. Didn't he tell you?'' Nick asked.

Mike stared at them. Then he looked to Caroline for some explanation, but all she could do was shrug.

''What crew? To do what?'' Mike asked.

Just then, the door opened and Jake and his brothers, plus Jim Randall and six other cowboys, piled into the office.

''Morning, Caro,'' Jake said, hugging his daughter. ''This is a bonus. I didn't know you'd be here.''

''I'm helping Jon check out the deputies before they begin their exercise regime,'' she answered.

''Hey, good thinking. Hi, Mike,'' Jake said, shaking his hand as his brothers had done.

''Did I miss something?'' Mike asked. ''I mean, did you say last night you were coming today? And why?''

''Well, I should have called you this morning, but I was afraid you wouldn't be up yet. Thought we'd just surprise you.'' He waved at the group of men around him. ''We're here to get started on our exercise room project.''

Mike frowned. ''But we're going to clean it up and

bring down the equipment I have. Then we'll be able to tell you what we've got room for. I'm sorry you came all this way for that. I'm not sure when we'll get it done."

"Son," Jake said, putting his hand on Mike's shoulder, "we're here to do some real work. Things are slow on the ranch in the winter. Toby keeps working in the arena training his horses, and two of the hands stayed with him. But the rest of us don't have much to do. So we're going to build you a bigger workout center."

Mike appeared stunned. "Build a new center? But that would cost money and take a lot of time."

Jake's brother Chad winked at him. "Everyone's pitching in so it won't take so long. Besides, Jim and I, in particular, have a debt to pay."

"No, Mr. Randall—I mean Chad—that's not necessary."

Pete grinned. "You just go ahead with whatever you're doing and we'll let you know if we run into snags."

The men all followed Jake's lead and walked into the storeroom, closing the door behind them.

Nick and Gabe still stood there, with grins on their faces. Gabe said, "I'm used to the way Jake and his brothers do business. Nick is still learning."

"Yeah," his twin agreed. "And we'd better catch up with them, because I'm the one who has building experience."

Mike looked even more confused. "But you're a lawyer."

"Yeah, but every summer for seven years I built houses to earn money for college."

Gabe smiled even more broadly. "Now, don't you start feeling sorry for him. His daddy had plenty of money. But he wanted his son to be well-rounded. I'm the one who grew up poor. Not old moneybags here." Both men laughed.

Mike was confused, and it must have shown on his face because Gabe launched into an abbreviated family history. He told Mike how their widowed young mother had given up Nick for adoption to a wealthy family with the resources to correct his club foot. Gabe had been raised by their mom until she died, when he was thirteen, at which point he'd left to follow the rodeo. It wasn't until after Nick's adoptive parents died that he'd found his twin in Rawhide.

Even families like the Randalls had their share of hardship, Mike thought as he watched them follow Jake into the back room.

When Jon came in moments later, he looked at Caroline and then Mike. "Anything wrong?"

He was carrying a doctor's scale. Mike reached to help him.

"Wrong? I guess not. I've just been invaded by Randalls."

Jon came to an abrupt halt and stared around him. "Where are they?"

"In the storeroom. I guess you and Caroline should set up in the snack room. That will at least give you some privacy. You'll need to start with my two night men. They're anxious to get home." He waved to a couple of deputies.

Caroline, delighted to move away from Mike, immediately carried her coffee to the snack room. Jon and Mike followed with the heavy scale. The two men Mike had mentioned followed.

Jon looked at the two deputies. "I'll take one of you and Caroline the other. You'll need to step on the scale and then unbutton your shirt."

Both deputies looked at Caroline skeptically, but she'd seen that reaction before. "I really am a doctor, gentlemen. Think nothing of it."

Then she turned her back to them to provide a little privacy until they adjusted to the idea.

"Boss, you gonna get checked?" one of them asked.

Caroline froze, waiting for Mike's answer.

"Nope. I'm not starting something new. Though I guess I could get my stitches removed, couldn't I, Doc?"

She turned to see if he was talking to her. Instead, he was looking at Jon.

"When did you get them?" Jon asked.

"The other doc put them in last Friday night."

The other doc? Was he going to pretend they didn't even know each other?

"What do you say, Caro?" Jon asked.

"The other doc says wait until next Monday."

Jon shrugged his shoulders. "Sorry, Mike."

"So I come in Monday morning?"

"If you call my office and make an appointment," she said crisply, not looking at him.

The back door opened. "Hey, Mike," Nick called. "Can you spare us a minute?"

"Sure, I'll be right there." After the door closed, he looked at Jon. "Everyone okay in here?"

"Sure," Jon said, sparing Caroline a sideways glance. "We're fine."

After Mike walked away, Jon leaned over and whispered to his colleague, "Did Mike and 'the other doctor' have a fight?"

"Of course not," Caroline replied. "We're just going to approach friendship more, um, cautiously."

"Okay," Jon agreed, his curiosity obviously not appeased.

A few minutes later, Mike returned, another dazed expression on his face.

Jon said something to him, but Caroline didn't pay attention. She was too busy trying not to laugh. The younger deputy had chosen to let her do his exam, and she was making bets with herself about how long he could go without breathing and letting out his gut. His endurance was impressing her.

"Now take a deep breath and hold it," she ordered softly.

He gave her a surprised look and took a small breath, still sucking in his stomach.

Mike, obviously paying close attention, walked by and ordered, "Breathe, you idiot!"

The man turned bright red.

"Don't pay him any heed," Caroline said gently. "You're doing fine."

This time the man actually relaxed, and she quickly repeated her examination. She and Jon each did two more exams, including Willie, who had been released from the hospital with a clean bill of health, but was still sure he would die if he did any exercise.

As they were finishing, Caroline said, "Each of you will lose some weight if you do the exercises regularly. It might be a good idea to weigh in once a week and keep a chart.''

Mike answered, "Good idea, Doctor. Willie, you can make the chart today. You'll start your schedule of exercises tomorrow, only doing half of your suggested program for the time being. We want to ease you into it.''

Willie didn't look pleased, but at least he didn't outright refuse.

"Did your meeting go well?'' Jon asked Mike.

Mike shook his head, and Caroline was amazed at how much she'd hoped he would be pleased with her family's efforts.

"It's just so much more than I expected. I was hoping they'd buy us another treadmill and maybe a better set of weights. But they're planning on building us an incredible facility.'' He looked at Jon. "Can you believe it? They want to put in showers, a sauna and a dressing room, in addition to the new equipment. I'm stunned. Jake said last night they'd take care of everything, but I had no idea what he intended.''

Caroline was tired of being in the doghouse. She leaned closer and said, "All the Randall men are stand-up guys.'' Then she closed her bag and walked out of the office.

Jon didn't follow. "You and Caroline get cross with each other?''

"Not exactly.''

"That doesn't tell me much,'' Jon pointed out.

"Well, I found out her problem, but...I think that's privileged information, even though I'd like your opinion. If she tells you, maybe we can talk.''

Jon frowned, suddenly worried. "It has to do with health?"

"Sort of."

Mike regretted his words immediately. The worry in Jon's eyes showed he wouldn't let it alone. Mike understood his concern. Before Caroline had explained her problem, he'd thought she might have a terminal illness. He'd wanted to grab her up, hide her in a cave and keep her all to himself for as long as they had.

Instead, he had to walk away from the most wonderful woman he'd ever met. He had to try to forget the incredible sex they'd shared. And he had to stop falling in love. So far he was doing a hell of a poor job of that particular item.

He had to put those thoughts away as Nick came back in with a sketch for the building project. Mike was afraid the Randalls would build the Taj Mahal if he didn't restrain them. Nick explained why they needed three showerheads, a dressing area and a sauna in addition to the weight room and the equipment to go in it.

"Nick, it isn't that I wouldn't like it. But don't you think it's going to be twice as expensive as what I asked for? How can I face everyone if I demand such a setup?"

"Open it up for the citizenry. You'll be the most popular sheriff in the world. Then I could come over here every morning and work out, have a cup of coffee, catch up on the news, all in one trip."

"Are you kidding?" Mike questioned.

"Nope."

"That's a deal, Nick. You and anyone else. There

will be certain times of the day that my men will have to have first preference so they can meet their schedules, but otherwise, it'll be open to the citizens of Rawhide.''

. ''That's great. I've gone to the high school gym before, but this will be more convenient. And a lot nicer. Gyms always have that smell.''

Mike laughed.

''By the way,'' Nick said, ''you and Caroline okay? You have an argument?''

''Why would you ask that?'' Mike didn't meet Nick's gaze.

''Jake asked me. I told him I'd ask you.''

''There's no problem,'' Mike assured him.

After Nick went back out to join the other Randalls and the cowboys, Mike tried to tell himself that. He and Caroline had no problems. Everything was fine.

He was actually coming to believe himself until the phone rang about two o'clock.

''Sheriff's Office,'' he said briskly.

A voice he recognized at once demanded fiercely, ''What the hell did you tell Jon?''

Chapter Nine

Mike drew a deep breath. "I told him I knew why you wouldn't marry."

"You told him?" Caroline demanded, her voice going up an octave.

"I didn't tell him the problem. I told him I knew what the problem was. Isn't that true?"

"Yes, but I expected you to keep quiet about it!"

"That's not easy, because one of your family questions me about our relationship every hour on the hour!" He was losing his temper. Taking a calming breath, he asked, "What did Jon say to you?"

"He wanted to give me a physical, and that's not necessary! There's nothing wrong with me!"

"I told you that!" Mike replied, his level of emotion rising again.

"Fine!"

"Fine!" In the silence that fell, he fought for control. "Caro, I want us to be together. Can't we try again?"

Silence.

Finally, she said, "I don't know. I need some time."

"Yeah, well, let me know."

CAROLINE KEPT HER HAND on the receiver after she'd hung up. What was she going to do?

"Caro, have you forgiven me?"

She looked up to see Jon standing in the doorway of her office. "I'm sorry I lost my temper. I didn't expect Mike to tell anyone." She cleared her throat. "The fact is that I can't have children. It makes me reluctant to commit to marriage. It's my experience that most men, even if they say they don't want children, eventually choose to have them."

"How do you know you can't have children?"

With a deep sigh, Caroline again recited the medical facts.

"But they may have changed. Four years is a long time."

Then she explained about Don.

"I'd still like to check."

"No, Jon. When I'm sick, you'll be the first one I'll call. But I'm not sick."

"Caro, can I tell Tori? We don't keep many secrets from each other."

Caroline covered her face. She hadn't wanted anyone to know, and now it appeared everyone would. Damn Mike! "Yes, of course."

Once Jon had left, Caroline spent a few minutes with her head on her desk, her eyes closed. She needed to think. Living without Mike seemed like a great sacrifice. She felt alive when she was with him. She felt safe when he held her. She—damn it! It hit her like the proverbial ton of bricks. She was in love. As she'd never been in love before.

And she wasn't sure Mike would even speak to her again.

She finally put her personal problems aside and got to the work that had carried her through everything. Her next patient was an elderly woman who complained that she couldn't move as fast as she used to. Caroline assured her that was normal for her age.

The lady slapped her hands away as Caroline tried to listen to her heart. "What's wrong with you, girl? I'm talking about being fast making Christmas presents. If I don't finish them before the twenty-fifth, my grandchildren will be disappointed!"

Christmas? Between dealing with the move and with Mike, Caroline had forgotten all about it. She hadn't bought one single Christmas present.

When the feisty old lady departed, Caroline called the ranch. Red answered the phone. "Hi, there, Caro. You coming out to see us?"

"I can't right now, Red. I'm between patients. But I haven't done anything for Christmas. I've got to talk to Mom and get busy."

"Aw, Caroline, just having you home is a good enough present."

"Thank you, Red. Tell Mom I'll call her tonight," she hastily said as her nurse signaled an emergency.

Caroline hurried around her desk and followed the nurse into an exam room. But she heard her patient before she got there. His screams of protest to his mother were deafening.

Gathering herself, Caroline entered the room, where the child's cries topped the decibel charts.

A towheaded boy of about seven sat in the corner, knees up, arms stretched in front of him, palms out.

A woman Caroline assumed was his mother squatted by him, no doubt trying to coax him out. She looked frantic, but it was obvious the boy wanted none of her cajoling.

"Get away from me!" he screamed at Caroline. "I wanna go home!"

She leaned a hip on the exam table, keeping her distance from the child, who was flushed—whether from crying or a fever, she didn't know. In a soothing voice, she reassured him, "I'm not going to do anything to you that you don't want."

The child stopped screaming, and his mother turned to look at her. "I'm so sorry. Zach just hates coming to the doctor."

"Hey, Zach," Caroline called, "would you like to examine *me* for a change? I'll even let you use my stethoscope."

The boy gave her a skeptical look, taking his time as he clearly pondered the offer. "You're not just trying to get me up there, are you?"

Caroline laughed. "No. I mean it." She flashed him a bright smile and extended her hand. "Come on. You may never get such a good offer again."

Zach looked at his mom, who nodded, then he got up and cautiously made his way to the table. He wiped his tears with the sleeve of his shirt and puffed up his chest. "Hop on up there, ma'am," he said in his best doctorly voice.

Choking back a chuckle, Caroline did as she was instructed.

Zach grabbed a throat swab from a jar on the cabinet and leaned in close to her mouth. "Now open wide so I can stick this Popsicle stick down your throat.''

"No, Zach!'' His mother screamed and lunged for him.

Caroline signaled for her to stay back. "You know, Zach, maybe I should show you how to do this properly. I know you don't want to hurt me." When he said okay, she had him open his mouth, and she gently, quickly wiped his throat with a sterile swab as she gave him verbal instructions. Then, though she questioned the wisdom in it, she let him do the same to her.

Surprisingly, the boy was just as gentle. He presented her with the stick. "You know, Doc,'' he said with a grin, "I know why you did that. You just wanted to get into my throat. But that's okay. It was worth it." His grin turned into a full-blown smile.

Nonplussed, Caroline just looked at him, her mouth agape. Bested by a grade-schooler.

"I'm so sorry, Doctor,'' the mother said, halfway between tears of embarrassment and of laughter. "Zach's quite a handful. From the day he was born he's been giving me and his daddy fits. There are days when I just can't win with him, but then there are those times when he does something so sweet…well, then I know he loves us." She cast a glance at him and smiled lovingly, her eyes glistening with tears. "His daddy and I wouldn't trade him for the world." She laughed. "Now I know what to get him for Christmas—"

"A doctor kit!'' the two women said simultaneously. Caroline smiled and went outside to give the swab to the nurse.

Zach's mom clearly had her hands full. But the boy was a charmer. Caroline thought about what the woman had said. Nobody could change what life had dealt them, could they? Even in frustrating or heart-breaking situations there was always that proverbial silver lining.

Even in my life? she thought. Where was her silver lining?

Minutes later she walked back in to the exam room and saw Zach on his mommy's lap, his little arms wrapped around her, hugging her tightly. And Caroline had her answer.

She'd been so focused on her woes, her fears, her shortcomings that she'd almost lost track of what was important in life. The people who loved her.

Had she stayed in Chicago all those years because she didn't have the courage to face them? This woman had no choice—she faced each day with her precocious son, never knowing how it was going to go, whether she'd pull her hair out in frustration or get one of these heart-squeezing hugs. But she woke up each day eager to see the outcome.

Caroline could have shaken herself for her weakness. She'd given up so much time with her family. She'd rejected an honest, good man who stirred her more than anyone she'd ever known. And she'd almost let the best holiday of the year pass by without a celebration. Not a celebration of material things, but a celebration of the richness of life.

This year she wanted a Christmas as raucous and joyful as the holiday would be at Zach's house.

She gave Zach's mom the good news of his negative strep test and wished them both a Merry Christmas. Then she invited Zach to come by the clinic anytime he wanted to lend his medical expertise.

"Dr. Randall, your mother is on the line." The nurse intercepted her as she left the room, and Caroline rushed to the phone in her office.

"Caroline, it's Mom. Red said you called. Is everything all right, dear?"

Was everything all right? It had never been better. "Yes, Mom. I just wanted to tell you that I'm glad to be home, so glad you didn't give up on me. And I'm sorry I didn't appreciate what you and Dad have given me."

"Sweetheart, what brought this on?"

"Let's just say a little boy helped me wise up." Her mother didn't even question the cryptic reply. "I need to do some quick Christmas shopping, Mom. I haven't bought a single gift yet."

"Well, we've taken to drawing names the past couple of years because there are so many of us. Everyone gets Red and Mildred something, of course. And immediate families exchange gifts."

"I haven't done any of that for four years. I'm so sorry."

"Don't be silly. I did it for you. Everything is just fine. Saturday, if you're off, we can drive to Casper and do a lot of damage."

"I'd love to, Mom." She wrote it in her calendar. "And, Mom, you and Dad like Mike, don't you?"

"Of course we do, darling. Why do you ask?"

"I'm attracted to him." It amazed her how easily she admitted the feeling. "And he doesn't seem to mind my…problem. I'd like to bring him to the ranch for Christmas—if he'll come."

"Of course. We were going to invite him, anyway."

"Can you keep Dad from insisting he marry me at once? That may not be what comes of our getting together."

"I'll try, but you know your father."

"Yes," she said with a laugh. "And that's what worries me."

"Caroline?" her mother said before hanging up.

"Yes, Mom?"

"Welcome home."

Patients needed to be seen, so her next call would have to wait. It wasn't until hours later that Caroline had a spare moment. She dialed the number.

"Sheriff's Office."

"Is Sheriff Davis in?"

"No, ma'am. Can someone else help you?"

She checked her watch and saw it was already five-thirty. "Has he left for the day?"

"Yes, ma'am. May I take a message?"

"No, thank you."

Sadly, she hung up the phone. Had she missed her chance? Her memories of falling asleep in his embrace, giving herself to him, were brief. She was greedy. She wanted more. But she wasn't going to feel sorry for herself. She had too much to do. Like shopping.

She put on her coat and headed for the general store. Nick's and Gabe's wives' emporium would make for a good start on her Christmas shopping. Besides, she hadn't seen Sarah and Jennifer Randall at all since she'd come home.

Caroline felt as if a weight had been lifted off her

shoulders. She had much to be grateful for. And now she was going shopping for her first Christmas in Rawhide in too many years.

"Caro?"

She found herself face-to-face with Tori. Jon's wife hugged her and Caroline felt a special urgency in the woman's embrace. "Uh-oh, Jon told you my problem, didn't he?"

"I'm so sorry."

Caroline smiled ruefully. "Don't feel bad, Tori. I've finally stopped feeling sorry for myself. And I want you to know I'm happy about your pregnancy." She lowered her gaze. "I'm just glad my family hasn't given up on me."

"What are you talking about? We would never do that!"

Caroline hugged her again. "I know. That's what I'm thankful for."

"I'm so glad you're feeling better about everything."

"Me, too. Someone told me I needed to get over it. And he was right. I'm off to do some Christmas shopping at the general store. Want to go?"

"Oh, I can't. I have to get home to—I mean, I need to—"

"It's okay, Tori. I know you have a baby. And I know you take good care of him." She cleared her throat. "Thanks for the support."

She walked briskly down Main Street, greeting residents as she went. Suddenly she was filled with the vibrancy of life.

In the store, she looked for gifts for her mother and father, Red and Mildred. The special people in her

life. When she bumped into a tall, denim-clad cowboy, she was surprised to recognize Harry.

"Are you Christmas shopping, too?" she asked the
deputy.

"Hi, Caroline," he said with a smile, but his gaze
continued moving over the store. "Uh, yeah."

"Need any help? I'm an expert on what women
like."

His cheeks turned bright red. "Nah, I can—do you
know that nurse? Susan?"

"Susan McAfee? Yes, I do. Pretty, isn't she?" she
teased.

"Yeah, I—I gotta go," he suddenly said, his voice
hardening. He moved swiftly toward the exit.

Caroline frowned, watching him as he stepped in
front of a man hurrying to the front door. She wasn't
close enough to hear what Harry said, but she recognized his technique as he spun the man around and
put him in cuffs. Mike Davis had clearly taught his
deputy well.

Sudden movement behind her caught Caroline's attention, and she swiveled around as Harry called to
someone. Another young deputy in civilian clothes
was struggling with a shopper. That deputy wasn't as
quick as Harry. The man got free and pulled a gun.
Caroline immediately yelled, "Gun!" and ducked
down between some shelves. Harry didn't hide. He
flew to his partner's assistance, getting there just in
time to draw fire away from the other deputy. Caroline grabbed a vase from the shelf and sneaked up
behind the man as he pointed his weapon again. She
cracked the vase over his head and he fell to the floor.
The deputy cuffed him.

She saw the manager of the store at the front door, holding on to the other cuffed man, who was trying to get out the door. Caroline rushed to the phone, called the Sheriff's Office for help, and Jon, too. Then she hurried to Harry's side.

"Hold still, Harry. Let me take a look at you."

"Caroline," he whispered. "Mike's going to be upset."

"Mike will be proud of you, as I am." She made a pad with a white towel she pulled off a shelf, and tried to slow the flow of blood.

Beside her the other deputy demanded to know if Harry would be all right. Then he kept muttering, "Sheriff is gonna kill me!"

The front door of the store burst open and Mike Davis quickly took in the situation. He was by Caroline's side in an instant. "Are you all right?"

"Yes, I'm fine. But we need to get Harry to the hospital and I don't have my vehicle here."

"Right. Hang in there, Harry," Mike said, reaching out and touching his shoulder. Then he left them again. In seconds he returned with a man he'd drafted to help carry Harry to his truck, which was waiting in the middle of Main Street, its motor running. Caroline followed.

Once they got Harry to the clinic, meeting Jon at the door, she scrubbed up while the nurses got Harry ready. Susan, the nurse Harry had mentioned, was on duty.

Caroline stopped by the young nurse. "Do you know Harry?"

"I met him a couple of weeks ago," she said from behind her mask.

"Do you need to be excused from the surgery?" Caroline asked gently.

"No! I want to help him."

Caroline nodded. She understood Susan's feelings. But it pleased her that the nurse showed some interest in Harry. Caroline was all for happy endings.

The operation took more than an hour, but when it was over, Caroline and Jon nodded at each other in relief. The bullet was out and Harry would be fine. The nurses took him to recovery and the two doctors stripped off their gloves and removed their masks.

"I'm glad you're here, Caroline. Together, we can provide excellent care for the people of Rawhide." Jon stretched his arms over his head. "Can't say the same for my back, though."

"Maybe we need to raise the table."

"That's a thought. We could get a table that we can raise or lower, like those chairs at the beauty salons." Jon frowned. "Why hadn't I thought of that?"

"I think it's because we accept what we're told." Hadn't she? In her own life she'd bought into everything Don had told her—with his cutting words and his betraying actions. That she was damaged goods. That no man would ever want her.

"Jon, I hope Tori told you I'm okay. I've counted my blessings."

"Good for you." He reached out and hugged her. "You know, I think Tori and I might give that special table to the clinic for Christmas. I'm going to look into that right away."

Caroline smiled. Then she stepped through the door to the waiting room. Immediately Mike, staring out a window, spun around and headed toward her. "How's Harry?"

"He's going to be fine. He'll have to stay here for a few days. Hopefully his boss will counsel him to follow his doctor's orders." She smiled, wishing she could touch Mike.

"Right," he said, but Caroline could see his mind was somewhere else. "Caroline, can you tell me what happened? The other deputy is babbling and I can't get the facts."

"Certainly," she said. "Shall we sit down?"

Mike frowned. "Okay. I assume I can't see Harry yet?" When Caroline shook her head, Mike took a seat on the sofa next to her.

"Don't worry. The nurses will let us know when he awakens." Caroline figured the best way to ease his concern was to give him the information he wanted. "I was in the general store doing some Christmas shopping. I saw Harry and was talking to him when he abruptly walked away."

Mike's gaze sharpened and he leaned closer. "And?"

"He went to the front door and intercepted a man hurriedly trying to leave. The man objected, but Harry deftly put him in cuffs. A move I've personally seen you make." She smiled and waited for a response, but he was focused on her story.

"The other deputy wasn't as…I mean, he had trouble with the second thief. At least I assume that's what he was. Harry realized his partner was in trouble and started toward them, pushing to the floor the man he'd cuffed."

"Harry wasn't shot at that point?"

"No. Harry did very well, Mike. You should be proud of him."

Mike nodded.

"I saw the second man pull a gun and I yelled 'Gun!' so Harry would be warned. The man was going to shoot the other deputy at point-blank range but Harry's rapid approach distracted him and he shot Harry instead."

"Steve—the other deputy—didn't get him cuffed?"

"Not until after I hit him on the head with a vase."

"I'm sorry you were involved. My men should have—"

"Don't be too hard on Steve. He knows Harry took the bullet for him."

"I won't be hard on him. But either he'll learn the job or he'll be looking for another one. I won't risk my men with someone who doesn't get it." Mike sat there for a minute, then he said, "Damn! I should've gone with Harry, but they might've recognized me!"

He stood and headed for the door.

"Mike?" she called, bringing him to a halt.

"Yes?"

"I'm glad Harry is safe."

He stared at her, and Caroline wanted to say so much more. But now wasn't the time.

"If Harry wakes up before I get back, tell him I'll be here as soon as I can."

MIKE WENT BACK to the Sheriff's Office, where most of his men were waiting for word on the fallen deputy. Everyone loved Harry, his enthusiasm and his sense of humor.

As soon as Mike entered the office, the men moved forward as one, asking questions.

He help up his hands. "The docs got the bullet out and say he'll be fine. He needs to stay in the hospital a few days, so we'll have to double up until he can come back to work. He..." Mike swallowed and cleared his throat. "He did exactly as he should've and did what he could for his partner."

The young man, hired only a couple of months ago, stood up, his body shaking from head to toe. "I—I know—I didn't—it's all my fault!" he finally wailed.

"Steve, you had some problems. It's not anything that you can't change. I'm going to step up some training procedures that would've helped you. You failed, but I failed you, too. Together, we'll get better."

"I can't—I don't know—"

"Now's not the time make any decisions, Steve. We all face the results of a critical mistake. In a few days, we'll start training. I want you to go home tonight and get some rest. Tomorrow you're assigned to the hospital, to wait on Harry and get him whatever he wants."

"Y-Yes, sir."

"And the rest of you need to let Harry know he did good. And you need to start our physical regimen, and get serious about it. Even you, Willie. Steve, I want weight lifting on your schedule. You're too lightweight right now."

"Yes, sir."

"All right, everyone go home, except for those on duty. Tomorrow is another day."

The men filed by him, shaking his hand, patting

him on the shoulder. When Steve waited until last, Mike knew he'd need more patience.

"Sheriff, I'm so sorry. I'd do anything—"

"Steve, every minute of training, every mile you run, every part of your job is what you can do to make up for today. But you're not alone. We're all going to be beside you. And don't forget your duty tomorrow. I expect to see you by Harry's bed."

"Yes, sir."

The young man dashed out the door and Mike gave a sigh of relief. He made for the door himself.

"You okay, boss?" one of his veterans asked.

"Yeah, Carmichael. Thanks for asking."

"I'm glad you came over to report. All those guys were driving me crazy. And hey, tell the docs we appreciate their work."

"Will do. Call if I'm needed."

Mike stepped out into the night air. He drew in a deep breath, hoping the cold could chase his thoughts away. He'd almost lost a man tonight. Damn, he was tired, but he owed it to Harry to be there for him.

Maybe he'd be able to thank Jon. He wasn't sure it was a good thing to face Caroline when he was feeling so low.

Taking another deep breath, he headed for the hospital.

Once inside, he was taken to see Harry. Mike entered the room, thinking his man would be alone. Instead, he found a couple of medical staff working on him.

"Hello? Is it all right if I—"

He stopped as Caroline faced him.

"Mike! I thought you'd gone."

"I had. My men needed to be reassured. But I wanted to see Harry before I went home."

"Of course. We were just adjusting a bandage for his comfort. Harry, the sheriff is here to see you."

Mike scarcely noticed the nurse standing there as he looked at his man. "How are you, Harry?"

"I'm okay, boss," the wounded man said in a weak voice. "I'm sorry—"

"No, Harry, you have nothing to apologize for. Everything's okay. We've got those guys in jail. You're a hero for saving Steve's butt."

"He's young," the wounded deputy murmured.

Mike smiled ruefully. Harry was all of twenty-five years old himself. "Yeah. Are you going to be able to sleep tonight?"

"Yep," Harry said. "I can hardly stay awake now."

"Then I'll say good-night. All the men will be by to see you in the next few days. And Steve will be your servant tomorrow."

"We can take care of Harry," the nurse said quickly.

Mike looked at her for the first time, hearing a possessive note in her voice. "Good. But Steve needs to work through his guilt."

She nodded, Harry had already closed his eyes and Mike decided his man was in good hands.

Mike realized suddenly that Caroline had disappeared. "Did the doctor go home?"

"Yes, sir," the nurse said. "She told us to call her if we needed anything. She was very tired." She seemed to be reprimanding him for demanding too much.

"Right," he said with a smile, and walked out of the hospital. Time for him to go home, too.

But his feet didn't take him home. Nor did they lead him to a phone to call Jon and express his gratitude. He'd do that tomorrow.

He didn't even admit to himself where he was going. Until he was standing in front of Caroline's door.

Chapter Ten

Caroline was trying to decide what to have for dinner when she heard a knock at the door. She hoped she didn't have to go back to the hospital. She was tired.

She swung the door open and discovered Mike standing there.

Frowning.

"Why did you open the door without asking who it was? That could be dangerous."

"Mike, this is Rawhide, not Chicago."

"Yeah. And Harry got shot today, so Rawhide isn't as innocent as it appears."

Caroline read the weariness in his eyes. She stepped back and gestured for him to come in. The surprise on his face told her she had some fence mending to do.

"I'd like to hear why that happened today," she said. "Obviously it didn't happen by chance."

Mike hesitated before he stepped over the threshold and allowed her to close the door against the cold. She'd lit a fire in the fireplace, making the room warm and inviting.

"If you'll sit down, I'll get us some coffee. I just

made it. I know you must be as tired as me. Did you get to talk to Harry?''

''Briefly.'' Mike sat down on the sofa and leaned his head back for a moment. Then he sat up and said, ''Did I hear a note of possessiveness in that nurse's voice?''

''I think so. Actually, Harry was asking me about her when he had to move to intercept that man. They were stealing, weren't they?'' She spoke from the kitchen as she poured the coffee.

When she came in with two mugs, Mike stood and took one from her. ''I don't care if I can't sleep. I needed this badly.''

''It's decaf,'' she assured him. ''How did you know they would be there?''

''We didn't know for sure. The manager called, explaining what he suspected. He'd been losing inventory. He began to realize that the loss of inventory occurred whenever a couple of men visited the store.'' With a shake of his head, Mike said, ''I offered to put some deputies in the store undercover.''

''Ah. That's why Harry was pretending to shop.''

''Yeah. I thought it would be a simple job. But when guns are involved, nothing is simple.''

''True.''

They sat there in silence, Mike watching the flickering flames of the fire, and Caroline watching him. Suddenly he stood up. ''I'd better go before I get too comfortable and fall asleep.''

''I was going to fix something to eat. It would be as easy to make it for two.''

''That's a very kind offer, but—''

"Mike, I want to tell you I...you woke me up when you yelled at me."

"I didn't really yell," he protested.

"You made me remember some things. I—I wanted to thank you."

"What are you saying, Caroline?"

He wasn't going to let her get away with subtlety. Okay, she owed him that much. "Mike, I'm over crying about my deficiencies. I've counted my blessings. And I'd like us to explore what was happening between us."

"You're sure?" he asked.

She stood and put her hands on his chest. "I'm sure. I already knew I was over Don. But now I'm through feeling sorry for myself. I have too much to be grateful for."

He covered her hands with his and dropped a gentle kiss on her lips. But he didn't prolong the contact. "I'm glad you understand how much you have to offer someone."

Caroline asked with a frown, "Someone?"

"Caroline, I'm attracted to you. You know that. But you're way out of my league. As you said, we lost control, but it's best forgotten. I just came by to thank you for taking care of Harry."

"I see," she said slowly, and withdrew her hands from his chest. Clearly, he didn't feel as she did. "Well, thanks aren't necessary."

"I think they are. Just like at the restaurant, you came to Harry's aid without hesitation. You even helped take down the bad guys. What are you doing? Trying to get a badge of your own?"

She couldn't take much more. Stiffly, she said,

"No, Sheriff, I'm not. Thank you for coming by." Then she walked to the door and opened it.

Mike stared at her, not moving. "Caroline, I'd like to be friends. We'll be working together a lot, apparently."

"Of course, Sheriff. After all, as you said, Rawhide is a small town. Avoiding each other would be hard work." She managed a smile, but it wasn't warm. How could it be? Her heart was breaking.

"Caroline—"

"I'm getting chilly, Mike," she pointed out, still standing by the open door.

He crossed to her side. "I'm still attracted to you, Caroline. I don't know a single red-blooded man who wouldn't be. But I'm just the sheriff, not a millionaire rancher or someone well known."

"I never asked you to be either of those."

"No, you didn't. Look, Caroline, I'm trying to do the right thing here."

"In your opinion," she pointed out, her jaw squared.

He raked a hand through his hair, confusion and frustration on his face. "Look, I'm not sure anymore what I think. The best I can say is we'll start again. Like we just met. Only I won't put you in cuffs, okay?"

"I'd appreciate that," she said, the ice around her heart melting a little.

"May I take you to dinner tomorrow night?"

"All right."

"Good. I've got to go. I'm going to jog at seven tomorrow so I can cover for some of the guys while they work out."

"Where do you jog?"

"I circle the town. Keep an eye on things while I exercise."

"I see. Well, thank you for coming over."

"I'll see you tomorrow night."

"Yes." To her surprise, he covered her lips with his and gave her a prolonged goodbye kiss. Then he left, reminding her to lock her door.

She did so and leaned against it. What was wrong with him? He was blowing hot and cold. His invitation to dinner and that goodbye kiss were hot. His hesitation and quick departure weren't.

Had she forced him to invite her to dinner? No. She'd accepted his obvious goodbye. He was the one who'd drawn back from the edge, who wanted to start over.

Okay. That meant he was fair game.

She checked her watch. She needed a quick dinner and an early bedtime. Because she was going to be out and about at seven in the morning!

MIKE HAD TOSSED and turned all night. He'd worried about Harry, worried about his misjudgment in assigning Steve to the case. He'd blamed himself for the team's failure.

And he'd worried about dating Caroline.

Man, he'd been a nervous wreck by the time he got out of her house last night. He'd wanted so badly to hold her close. If he were honest, he'd admit that he'd wanted to take her to bed. Instead, he was going to go slow, to date her.

His footing was unsure with Caroline, unusual for a decisive man like him. One minute Mike considered himself not rich enough for her blood; the next he knew himself to be a successful man whom people respected. One minute he thought she had issues with her own self-esteem and was pushing him away; the next she was coming on to him. Yes, about the only thing he knew for sure was that he wanted to be with her—however he could. As a friend. As a lover. Whatever way Caroline would allow.

Lord have mercy, she was going to try his patience. He'd have to be careful around her until he knew for certain where she was leading him.

He dressed in thermal jogging clothes. Then he did his stretching in his apartment. He added a small gun holster at the small of his back, just in case. Finally ready, he stepped outside and began his regular tour of the town.

That very quickly changed.

A lady with a long brown ponytail and a slim body, one he celebrated in his dreams, jogged to his side.

"Morning, Mike!"

"Caroline, what are you doing here?"

"Trying to keep in shape. I like to jog, but not alone. I hope you won't mind if I join you?"

He almost groaned aloud. Oh, yeah, that would get his heart working overtime, following her trim behind all over town. "Of course I don't mind."

She gave him a big smile and gestured for him to continue, then moved up beside him.

Somehow he'd thought she would try to carry on a conversation, but she was quiet, running easily beside him. It was clear she'd jogged before. "Did you jog in Chicago?" he asked her.

"When I could."

"With that guy?" Mike didn't look at her. He didn't want her to see the jealousy in his eyes.

"Don? No. He never jogged."

"Oh. Say, do you know that person?" Mike pointed out a man lingering in front of a store that was closed. The stranger served as a good distraction.

"Yes. That's John Miller. He's a farmer who lives south of town."

"Okay. I usually turn here and head down your street."

"Great."

Was she going to stop when they got to her house? After not wanting her to jog with him, he realized that should please him. But now he wanted her beside him. It seemed so natural, as if they'd jogged together for years. So comfortable.

When they reached her house, she made no move to stop. Mike released a big breath. It shouldn't have been so important, he told himself. He was overdoing it again. Just when he'd promised he'd take it slow. Right.

Caroline's voice interrupted his thoughts. "I'm going to Casper Saturday to do some shopping. Is there anything I can bring back for you? Or do you want to come? Mom and I are going to spend the day there."

It was tempting. But after yesterday's disaster, he couldn't afford to take off. "I'm going to do some training classes on Saturday. I don't want to put it off, after last night."

"You can't work every day," she protested. "You'll burn out."

He didn't answer for a minute. Then he said, "I'll

take some time off later. But we need to make some improvements.''

''Okay. So if you need some presents for Christmas, you can make me a list and I'll pick the things up.''

''You'd do that?'' he asked, surprised.

''Of course. We're friends, aren't we?''

''Yeah.'' That required another deep breath. Okay, so she'd bought his line about being friends. Well, it wasn't actually a line; it was more a beginning. A point he'd passed the first time he'd met her. But her response proved that he'd taken the right approach. At least she wasn't turning away.

''I'll have to think about a list. I might take you up on that offer.''

''Good.''

After jogging for forty-five minutes, they did a five-minute cooldown that took them back to the Sheriff's Office. But Mike passed it and finished at the door of Caroline's house.

''Thanks for joining me. It's nice to have a partner.''

''If it doesn't bother you, I'd like to join you every morning. I've been worried about setting up a routine.''

''I'd enjoy the company.''

She gave him a warm smile. ''Good. Oh, and where are we eating tonight?''

''I thought we'd go back to Le Mouton Bleu again. Hopefully, this time we can actually eat there.''

''Lovely. So I'll see you at…seven?''

''Let's make it six-thirty. I'll make the reservation for seven.''

She nodded in agreement and, smiling, went into her house.

Mike stood there in the cold. Finally he forced himself to go back to his office. He'd used his shower time to moon over Caroline.

CAROLINE DIDN'T THINK she was irresistible, but she knew the more time she and Mike spent together, the more likely it was that he'd become attached to her. And she was going to do everything she could to help that feeling along.

As she worked, she planned her appearance for that night. She wanted to tempt him…just a little. The afternoon was busy, but she managed to head for her house just after five.

Tonight deserved a bubble bath. It would clear her head and perfume her skin. Then she intended to put on a black dress, the slinkiest one she owned. No pants tonight. And even with snow on the ground, she intended to wear high heels.

She put her lipstick on at six twenty-five. She looked the best she could, she decided. Not too bad.

When six-thirty came and went, she frowned. Where was the man? She'd worked hard to bowl him over, but she couldn't do that if he didn't show up. At six-forty she began pacing.

When the phone rang, she pounced on it, but paused to take a deep breath. Then she calmly said, "Hello?

"Caroline, I'm sorry. I'll be right there. Oh, and, slight change of plans. We, uh, we're going to double-date."

She took a deep breath. Double-dating didn't fit in with her expectations. "Why?"

"You'll understand when I get there." And he hung up.

Caroline was not happy. He'd just ruined all her plans.

She paced the floor again, regretting all her preparations.

She'd just decided to change into slacks and a sweater when there was a knock on her door. Shrugging her shoulder, she went over and threw it open.

"Sheriff!" she exclaimed, smiling. She wasn't speaking to Mike. She was greeting Bill Metzger.

He gave her a big bear hug. "How are you, Caro? I was glad to hear you finally came home."

"I'm glad, too. How are you feeling? Mike said you had a heart attack."

"Yeah. But I've found out it was minor. I've been exercising and I'm getting stronger."

"That's wonderful!"

"Uncle Bill, we're already late," Mike interjected. "We'd better go pick up Margie, or she'll think we're not coming." He looked at Caroline, and she realized Margie Dunster was going with them. Definitely a double date.

Mike took her arm after she locked the door, and led her to his vehicle. Bill had gotten in the back seat, and Mike put her in front. As she started to slide in, he whispered, "I'm sorry about this. You look terrific."

She gave him a smile, but it wasn't a happy one.

When they reached Margie's house, she and Mike remained in the SUV while Bill went to get his date.

"You didn't know he was coming?" she asked quietly.

"I had no idea. He wants his job back."

"What? No, he can't—"

"He can. And the ranchers will back him. They're all old friends."

"I'm sure they'll be glad to see him, but he shouldn't be allowed to take your job. We need someone young like you to inject some energy, some new ideas."

Mike shook his head. "I made a big mistake yesterday. I doubt if anyone will back me. Even if they did, how could I turn my uncle away? If he wants the job, it's his."

And she thought her plans had been ruined before!

Bill and Margie Dunster reached the SUV arm in arm, happy smiles on their faces. He leaned over and kissed her just before they got in the SUV.

After the greetings, silence fell as Mike sped out of town toward Buffalo. Lost in quiet thought, Caroline decided to call her father. She wasn't willing to accept the end of Mike's job in Rawhide. She thought he was good for the town. Even if Bill wanted his job back, surely something could be done. And her father was the one to do it.

They were warmly welcomed at the restaurant by the maître d', who obviously remembered them. When they sat down, Bill asked what was going on. Caroline stood. "I'll let Mike explain our adventure while I excuse myself."

Mike gave her a curious look, but she only smiled and headed for the ladies' room. Inside, she sat down on a couch and pulled out her cell phone.

Red answered and Caroline asked for her father. In seconds, Jake Randall was on the phone.

"Dad, Bill Metzger is back in Rawhide. He has been exercising and thinks his health is greatly improved." She took a deep breath. "He wants his old job back."

There was a moment of silence. Then Jake got to the heart of the problem. "What does he expect Mike to do?"

"I don't know. But Mike said he couldn't fight his uncle."

"I can imagine that, and I'm glad he feels that way, but I don't think that's a good idea."

"Neither do I. Is there anything I can do?"

"Well, you could marry him."

"Dad! I'm being serious."

He chuckled. "Me, too!" Then he cleared his throat. "I'll talk to the family and see what we can do. Will you tell Mike to hold on for a couple of days?"

"Yes. If he'll listen to me."

"Give it your best, sweetheart. He's a good man and we want him to stay."

"So do I."

BILL PUSHED BACK from the table. "That was a mighty fine meal."

"Yes," Mike agreed. "It was very good. How about some dessert?"

"Ooh! I'd love some," Margie said. "I just love French desserts. Those little fruit tarts. I'm sure they can't be fattening, they're so small."

The older woman had been downright giddy with

happiness. Before Bill's heart attack, they had had a comfortable relationship that no one talked about but everyone knew was happening. Once he was gone, she'd been lonesome.

"Sure, we'll have dessert if you want it, Margie. And a bottle of champagne," Bill ordered from the waiter hovering near.

"Champagne?" Mike asked. "Are we toasting something?"

"I'll let you know in a minute. Margie, I've missed you so much. Now that I'm better and I don't think doing—well, you know what I mean. I want to marry you. Will you accept my proposal?"

Margie screamed, leaped from her chair and threw her arms around Bill's neck, plopping down in his lap. "Yes, yes, yes! Oh, Bill, I thought I'd lost you. I've been so lonely."

She gave him a big kiss. Then she asked, "When?"

"Right away! I'm going to be sheriff again."

"You mean I don't get to move to Arizona?"

There was a flicker of hope in Caroline's heart, but it was quickly doused when Bill told her she wouldn't like Arizona. "We're going to be here. I'm going to be sheriff again. We'll be here with our friends."

Caroline looked at Mike, but he kept his gaze on the table and said nothing. But it wasn't fair! Bill Metzger wasn't thinking about Mike. He was casting him aside as if the change Mike had made in his life meant nothing.

Now Mike would return to Chicago. And she'd be left behind.

Chapter Eleven

Mike had offered Bill his apartment—soon to be Bill's—to stay in. Instead, he asked Mike to pick up his suitcase and take it to Margie's house.

"My boxes should be here in a couple of days," he added.

Mike nodded and said nothing.

After the couple got out and disappeared into Margie's house, Mike drove in silence. Caroline didn't speak till he parked beside her house. "I called Dad. He said for you to hang on for a couple of days and he'd see what he could do."

"Caroline, I can't do that. He's like my father. After my dad died, Bill was there for me. I can't oppose him."

"So you've decided to go back to Chicago?"

"If they'll take me. If not, I'll have to find a police force that needs help."

Caroline sat there, fighting tears. "So our… friendship doesn't matter?"

"Caroline, there's nothing I can do! I don't want to go to Chicago. I don't want to give up my job when I'm just getting started, but I have no choice." He gave her a hopeful look. "Didn't you want to return to Chicago?"

"No. I've finally found my way home, and I have no desire to go back there. Mike, don't go, please!" She reached for him, wrapping her arms around his neck.

"Honey, I don't have a choice."

"Maybe Dad can—"

"I told you I won't fight Bill on this. I'll be leaving as soon as possible."

She pulled away from him. "I guess I overestimated your interest. Good night, Mike." She opened the door and jumped out, running to her house.

Mike called her name and she heard him get out of the truck, but she couldn't take any more. He wasn't even going to try to keep his job. It was hopeless.

MIKE GOT UP and prepared to do his normal jogging at seven. Secretly, he hoped Caroline would join him again. He didn't want to leave her. But he had no choice.

She didn't appear. He jogged past her house twice, slowing down each time. No sign of life. When he got back to the office, he went upstairs to the apartment and showered. When he came down, he was pleased to see a couple of his deputies working out. But he supposed that program would be canceled.

On his run, he'd seen some of the men from the Randall ranch come to work, and he could hear sawing and hammering in the back. There was no sign of Bill yet. Mike knew he had to prepare his men for the change.

"I'm going over to see Harry," he told one of the deputies. "Have everyone hang out here until I get back."

"Yes, sir."

He reached the clinic, knowing Caroline wouldn't be there yet. He found Harry's room. "How you doing?"

"Fine, boss," he said, sounding almost normal. "But you gotta put Steve back to work. He's driving me and everyone else here absolutely crazy."

"Is he already here?"

"Yep. Susan sent him off on a task—" Harry nodded to the nurse at his bedside "—but he'll be back anytime."

"I'm sorry he's a problem. I'll get him back to the office."

"Thank you," the nurse said.

"You're Susan?" Mike asked.

"Yes."

"Thanks for taking such good care of Harry."

She gave him a shy smile. "I have a vested interest." Her cheeks reddened. Harry reached out and took her hand.

Mike grinned. It was good to see that someone would have a happy ending. "Would you mind if I speak to Harry alone for a minute?"

"Of course not," she quickly said, and excused herself.

Harry immediately asked, "What's wrong?"

"Nothing for you. My uncle has come back."

"Sheriff Metzger?" Harry asked in surprise.

"Yes. He's doing much better and he wants to be

sheriff again. I just thought I'd let you know of the change that's about to happen."

"You're giving up your job?" Harry asked, his voice rising. "You can't do that, boss. You were going to teach us a lot. Make life better here!"

"Yeah, and I did such a good job, I got you shot."

"Hell, that wasn't your responsibility. Steve just isn't as seasoned as he should be."

"And who decided Steve should participate in that undercover operation?"

"Me. I suggested Steve and I should work it."

"I appreciate your answer, Harry, but Uncle Bill is going to take his job back. I just wanted to prepare you."

"Can't you fight him?"

"He's like a father to me. I can't do that."

"Damn."

"I'm going now. I'll get Steve back to the office and save you from his guilt. And I'll come see you before I leave."

Mike stepped out of the room and almost bumped into Caroline. "Whoa!" he said as he caught her arms to steady her balance. "Sorry, I didn't see you coming."

"How is Harry?"

"He's improving rapidly. Enough to complain about Steve's guilt. I'm taking the rookie back to the office with me."

"Good."

"Are you doing okay?"

She stiffened. "Why wouldn't I be?"

So she was going to act as if nothing had happened

between them. Okay. "No reason. I'm going to find Steve. Thanks again for Harry's quick recovery."

She nodded, but she wouldn't look at him. With regret, he strode down the hall. Damn. He was giving up a lot leaving Rawhide.

When he got back to the office, his uncle was there, sitting at Mike's desk. Mike fought the urge to unseat him. Instead, he smiled and welcomed him back. "Have you talked to the men?"

"No. Gary said you wanted everyone to wait until you got here."

"Yeah. You haven't changed your mind, have you?"

"Nope. I'm delighted to be back."

Mike turned to go speak to the men, and came face-to-face with Jake Randall. "Hi, Jake. How's the project going?"

"Really well."

"What's going on, Jake?" Bill asked, getting up to shake his hand. "It's good to see you."

"Good to see you, too, Bill. But what's this about you coming back to work?"

"Yep! I'm just about recovered. Me and Margie are gonna get married and I'll have another twenty years here."

"What about Mike?" Jake asked.

Mike started to protest, but the rancher gave him a look clearly asking for silence.

"Why, I guess he'll go back to Chicago. I'm sure they'll take him on again."

Jake glanced at his friend. Then he turned to Mike. "Leave me with your uncle. And don't say anything to the men."

Mike frowned. "Look, Jake, it's Uncle Bill's choice."

"Not necessarily. Go."

Mike saw his uncle begin to question Jake about his meaning, but he didn't wait to hear the discussion. He closed the door behind him as he went out.

"Hey, Mike, what's going on in there?" Willie asked.

"I'm not sure."

"Is it true Bill's coming back? I guess that means I don't need to do those stupid exercises. Bill wouldn't ask that of me."

The man's attitude angered Mike, but he held his temper. Until Jake and Bill had talked, who knew what would happen? He couldn't help but hope something could be worked out that would leave him some kind of a job in Rawhide.

CAROLINE CALLED her mother at lunchtime, anxiously wanting to hear what her father was going to do. But B.J. wasn't at home.

"She's working today, child," Mildred said.

"Oh. Have you heard from Dad? Is he working at the jail?"

"Sure is."

"Good. I'll go over there."

She'd go on the pretext of inviting her dad to lunch. Surely he wouldn't let Mike be sent away. She hoped.

She didn't know if she and Mike were destined to share a life, but if they were, it certainly wasn't working out easily. Especially if he refused to fight for their future.

She gathered up her new beeper, which had arrived

the day before. Then she talked with one of the nurses and went to check on Harry.

"Caroline? Have you heard anything about Mike leaving?" Harry asked at once.

"Yes."

"Isn't there something we can do? I like Sheriff Metzger, but Mike's so good."

Caroline slowly shook her head. "He won't oppose his uncle, Harry. So there's nothing we can do, as far as I know. I did tell my father last night. Maybe he'll be able to change their minds."

"If there's anything I can do, just let me know."

"I will, Harry. I'm going to go meet my dad now."

"I'll keep my fingers crossed."

She gave him a brief smile and hurried out the door. She couldn't think of a better man than her father to keep Mike here. Except for Mike himself.

She hurried to the Sheriff's Office. What if her father wasn't there? What if he'd given up, or had decided to support Bill? What if Mike was already packing?

She opened the door with trepidation.

The first thing she saw was Mike, sitting at one of the desks. Why wasn't he in his office? She looked at the closed door. "Is my dad in there?"

"Yes," he answered, his voice clipped and unemotional.

Caroline debated her options. Finally she walked to Mike and pulled out a chair. "What's going on?" she asked in a quiet voice.

"I don't know. Your dad shut me out and they haven't opened the door for almost two hours. But we haven't heard any gunshots or yelling, so I assume they're both okay.''

"Are my uncles here?"

"They're working out back, I believe."

Caroline got up and headed for the back room.

"Caroline?" Mike called.

"Yes?"

He didn't respond at first. Then he said, "Never mind."

Through the door, Caroline found a new world. They had knocked out the original walls and were quickly putting up new ones, making a much bigger room.

Everyone greeted her.

"Uncle Pete, may I speak to you?"

"Sure, Caro. There's not anything wrong at home, is there?"

"Oh, no. Everything's fine."

She waited until Pete got close to her. "I don't want anyone to hear, but what did Dad decide to do about...the sheriff?"

"We all thought it would be good to keep Mike and to talk Bill out of his decision."

Caroline let out a big breath. "Oh, that's good. Do you think he'll be able to do that?"

"We hope so. We all like Bill, but we need a younger sheriff. Mike brings a lot of skill and energy to the job."

"Mike won't fight Bill. He says he's been like a father to him."

"We understand that, but I think he likes it here. We're trying to work something out."

"Good." She hugged her uncle and kissed his cheek. "Thank you so much."

"No problem, Caro. We're all waiting to see if Jake makes progress."

"How much longer do you think it will—"

"Caro?" Jake called.

Caroline whirled around and ran to her father's arms. "Dad! What happened? Did you work things out?"

"I think so."

"Is Sheriff Metzger leaving?"

"No, I don't think so." As Caroline gasped, Jake hurriedly added, "I think he'll leave Mike as sheriff, though."

"But what would he be?"

"That's what he and Mike are talking about now."

"Mike said he'd be going back to Chicago."

Jake grinned. "If he does, it will be because he wants to go. Bill's going to make that clear."

Caroline gave a silent prayer of thanks and kissed her father's cheek. "I came to take you to lunch. Can you go?"

"Of course I can, if you're buying!" He grinned at her.

"Oh, yes. I owe you big time."

She knew she couldn't celebrate until she heard Mike's decision. She should've gotten her head straight earlier, and should have talked to him about her feelings, she decided with a pang of regret.

"Okay," Jake said. "Lunchtime, guys!" he called out. "Caroline's buying. Everyone to the café!"

When he winked at his daughter, letting her know

he was teasing, she shook her head. "It's worth it, Dad."

"No, you need to save your money. I always buy lunch, anyway. Let's go see if Mike and Bill want to join us."

"Do you think we should?" Caroline asked, thinking of that closed door.

"Yeah. I'm not prepared to wait any longer."

Caroline wasn't, either.

As all the men, including her uncles, began putting away their tools, Jake took her arm and led her to the big room where several deputies were working. The door to the Sheriff's Office was still closed.

Jake strode over and gave a brief knock. Then he opened it. "We're extending an invitation to lunch. My daughter has promised to treat. Anyone interested?"

Bill gave Jake a rueful look. "I'm supposed to be at Margie's for lunch. You try to convince my best man to keep his job." Shaking his head, he exited the Sheriff's Office.

Caroline's heart sank.

Jake glanced at her. "Give me a minute with Mike."

Caroline watched as her dad went in and closed the door behind him.

JAKE STARED AT MIKE. "So, you're going to abandon my daughter?"

"Sir, your daughter told me she only wanted us to be friends. That's the kiss of death, and you know it."

Jake grinned. "Yeah, that's a killer. So you think

my daughter asked me to help because she's concerned about law enforcement in Rawhide?''

''Probably.''

''Mike, wake up. Not only does she not want you to leave, but your uncle doesn't, either. Didn't he tell you that?''

''Sure. But you didn't see how excited he was about coming back.'' Mike rubbed the back of his neck. ''Look, Jake, the man's been good to me. I can't take the job he wants.''

''He's not being offered the job.''

''What?''

''We're all glad he's back, but not as sheriff. We want you as the sheriff. We like your energy, your superior training, your heart.''

''Sir, if you're arguing this because you think Caroline will decide she wants to marry, I can't promise—''

''Mike, I want you because you believe in not using guns without just cause. And you want to raise the entire staff to that level. I approve.''

''But Caroline—''

''I'm not demanding anything from you on the subject of Caroline. I want her happy, but only if the man feels the same way.''

Mike stood and stuck out his hand. ''Thank you. I accept.''

Jake took it in his. ''Let's go eat.'' He clapped Mike on the back as they stepped out into the main office.

Caroline sat behind a desk. ''Everyone else is gone.''

"Then we'd better hurry," Jake said. "I don't want the café to run out of enchiladas."

"Are you eating with us?" she asked Mike, keeping all emotion from her face and voice.

"I do love enchiladas," he said with a grin.

Caroline stood up and put her hands on her hips. "Mike Davis, I have worried myself sick about you losing your job and having to go back to Chicago, and you want to make jokes?"

She didn't wait for an answer. She strode out of the office. "I'm going home."

When someone caught hold of her arm, she whirled around again, ready to start swinging. Only it was her father.

"Whoa, Caroline. You're not the only one who's been through a lot this morning. Pull yourself together, because you're going to join us whether you want to or not. All the guys will think you're mad about buying lunch. I won't have that."

Caroline bowed her head, trying to compose herself. "Of course, Dad. I apologize. I hope we can find three places to sit." She began walking at a more moderate rate. Her father was right. She couldn't hurt the feelings of all the men working so hard to give Mike what he wanted.

Before she entered the café, she pasted a smile on her face. She didn't look to see if Mike was still with them. She told herself she didn't care. She was going to make her father proud.

When she went inside, she found all the men seated at tables side by side. She stopped the waitress who was serving them. "I hope they told you I was paying," she said.

"Yes," the woman said, "but I didn't want to take their word for it until I saw you."

"It's true. And don't let them skip dessert, either. They've earned it."

The men, overhearing her, cheered.

Her father stepped past her. "I'm joining my brothers. There's a table for two over there. You'd better go grab it," he said, looking at Mike.

"Dad!" Caroline protested.

But her father just smiled and walked away.

Mike took her arm and headed for the small table for two in a corner. "Come on, sit down. If you do, I'll split the bill with you."

Bitterly, she whispered, "Do you think I care about that? Do you think that's why I yelled at you?"

"No, I think you're frustrated...as I am. I'm staying, Caroline. That's what I wanted. But I couldn't do anything to hurt Uncle Bill. You want to know what we worked out?"

"Yes," she admitted, but her voice was shaking.

As he sat down, a waitress came to wait on them. "Could you bring us a couple of coffees at once? It's cold out there."

"Of course, Sheriff. Right away." The woman didn't even wait for Caroline to say anything.

"I'm glad that's what I want," she said softly.

Mike grinned. "If it's not, I'll personally have it changed. I appreciate your support, Caroline. I appreciate your father's negotiation skills. I didn't want to leave town."

Caroline swallowed. "So, what did you work out?"

"Your father pointed out that if Bill wanted to live

another twenty years and enjoy his marriage, he needed a less stressful job.''

"What job?" Caroline could hardly wait to hear.

"We'll share the work, but Bill will focus on the administrative side. I'll be in charge of training and working with the men. Jake said he'd make sure they had enough money to pay for another administrator. I was afraid Bill wouldn't be able to handle that change, but he was pleased. He said he knew he couldn't meet the standards I was setting. He thought my idea was good, especially since it'll be implemented with an incredible workout facility.''

"And that's all it took?"

"He wanted the job again so he could provide for Margie. And he'll earn his money. The paperwork is copious, believe me. If there's time, I can help him out. If other things are going on, he can handle it on his own.''

The waitress brought their coffee. Caroline took a sip to steady herself. "I'm so glad it worked out."

"Yeah. Do I dare ask you out to dinner again?"

"Maybe we should plan on eating in. We'll—oh, dear. I've already made plans to leave this evening for Casper with my mother. I won't be back until late Saturday night."

"How about dinner Sunday evening?"

"All right. But I'll cook. And if you show up on my doorstep with anyone else, I'm not going to let you in."

"That sounds promising. Will you dress like you did last night?"

"You noticed?"

"You know I did, Caro. I'd have to be dead not to notice."

She couldn't hold back a smile. Then she said, "Oh! Harry. I told him you were leaving. He was very upset."

"He wasn't the only one. We've become good friends. I'll go with you to the hospital to reassure him."

Chapter Twelve

Mike did want to tell Harry that he was staying, accompanying her to the clinic also meant he could remain in Caroline's company a little bit longer. He felt that he'd averted disaster with his uncle's offer to stay here as the administrative sheriff while he ran the department. It was the best of both worlds.

He'd have family here with him, and he'd be close to Caroline. How close might be determined Sunday night.

They walked slowly back to the hospital, trying to extend their few private minutes.

"I missed you jogging with me this morning."

"I wasn't sure you'd go with so much happening."

He shrugged his shoulders. "Got to stay in shape."

"I'm glad you're staying," she whispered, as if afraid someone might hear her.

"Me, too. So we get our chance to start over?"

"Sunday night."

"I'll see you then."

At the door of the clinic they each went their separate ways, with covert back glances.

Mike stepped into Harry's room without knocking

and interrupted a kiss Harry was sharing with the nurse, Susan.

Mike coughed, which had the two lovebirds jumping apart. "Excuse me. Didn't mean to interrupt anything."

Susan hurried to the door, saying nothing.

When they were left alone, Harry said, "Don't tell me you've come to say goodbye, 'cause I can't take that. You're too good."

Mike smiled at his deputy and friend, and told him the news.

"Thank God," Harry said with relief, holding out his left hand to shake Mike's in congratulation.

"Thanks, Harry. I'm happy about it, too. I get to keep my job and have Uncle Bill here."

"And you get to hang out with Caroline?" Harry teased.

"Harry, my friend, at least I wasn't caught smooching."

Harry turned a bright red. "Don't tell anyone, boss. I don't want Susie embarrassed. She's special!"

"Good. Maybe we can give you a raise so you can support her."

"We haven't gotten that far. Marriage is a big step."

Mike felt as if a mirror had been held up to his thoughts. "I know what you mean, Harry, but when the right woman comes along, you don't want her to move on. Susan seems like she might be the right woman."

"Is that because you think Caroline is the right woman for you?"

"It's possible. But there are complications. When

you're older, you've got a lot of baggage you haven't unpacked," he added with a grin. To change the subject, Mike asked, "Is there anything you need?"

"Nope. Steve came by on the way in this morning to offer to do anything. Everyone in the hospital cringes when he comes in the door. It's like kicking a puppy when I can't think of anything he can do for me. This morning I told him I needed a paper so I could see what's going on in the world. I think he ran all the way to the newsstand and brought me back the *Chicago Sun-Times.*"

Mike grinned. "That's what you get for being a hero."

Harry blushed. "I'm not a hero."

Mike turned serious. "Harry, did you not use your gun because of things I've said? You could've shot the thief before he shot you, I believe."

Harry gave him a rueful smile. "Nope. I just didn't think fast enough."

Mike patted him on the shoulder. "Okay. But if only a gun will work, don't hesitate to use it."

"Yes, Sheriff," Harry agreed, grinning. "I'm so glad I can still call you that."

"Me, too."

CAROLINE WAS ENJOYING her trip to Casper. In addition to her mom, her aunt Janie and Toby's wife, Elizabeth, had come along.

"Wow!" Elizabeth said as they drove to another store. "A weekend without the kids! What a great idea."

The two other mothers laughed. Caroline stared at

Elizabeth. "You're happy to be without your children?"

"Don't look so horrified, dear," her mother said. "When you were little, I enjoyed time away, too."

"Oh, lordy, yes," Janie agreed. "It was like the twins had sixteen arms and legs, all finding trouble."

Everyone laughed. But Caroline still looked concerned. "Don't you worry about them while you're away?"

Still laughing, Janie said, "Every minute of every day, whether I'm there or not. But we're lucky. We have Mildred and Red. And when Pete and I went to Hawaii, we had Camille and Griff. Of course, we didn't know then they would end up married to each other."

"But if you worry about the kids, why does it make you feel good to go away?"

"Because we know we're coming back," Elizabeth said. "And they always miss us. But not too much. It's humbling to see how happy they are with Red and Mildred. But that hug they keep just for you is special. We come home refreshed and they appreciate us more."

"Nicely said, Elizabeth," B.J. exclaimed.

"You'll see," Janie added, "when you have your own little ones."

Caroline didn't run away and hide this time. "Probably not, Aunt Janie. They don't think I can have children." She knew even her mother was surprised by her openness.

Janie broke the silence. "Oh, honey, I'm sorry. I shouldn't have said that."

"You didn't know, Aunt Janie. It's all right. I'm

over feeling sorry for myself. I have a lot to be thankful for.''

Since Caroline was driving and her mother was riding in the back seat, B.J. simply said, "I'm proud of you, Caro."

"Thanks, Mom," she replied, smiling at her mother in the rearview mirror.

"Why didn't you tell us?" Elizabeth asked, sympathy in her voice.

"Because for four years now, I believed I was damaged goods, that I didn't have anything to offer a man. And the bum I was living with did nothing to change my mind. Especially when he left me for his nurse, who happened to be carrying his child."

"He deserves to be lynched!" Janie said, and the others agreed.

They drove in silence for a couple of minutes until Elizabeth asked another question. "So what made you realize you're *not* damaged goods?"

Caroline smiled. "Someone told me to get over feeling sorry for myself. I started counting my blessings. Top on the list is my wonderful family."

"You definitely are right," Janie said with a laugh.

MIKE WAS COUNTING the minutes until Caroline got back and he could show up on her doorstep. He hoped no one noticed his distraction. He kept telling himself he'd take it slow. But he was haunted by memories of the one night they'd spent together.

The training session he'd conducted yesterday had gone well. He'd taken three of the youngest deputies, Steve included, and taught them how to handle perps, even if the bad guys were bigger than them. And

Mike was making sure his men were doing their exercises. One of Bill's administrative duties was to record the amount of time each one exercised.

Mike went upstairs and showered and changed when it was close to time to go to Caroline's. Then he came back down to the Sheriff's Office. "I've got my beeper with me if you need me tonight," he told the guys on duty.

"You smell mighty purty for an old sheriff!" one of his men declared.

"Too much?"

"Naw, I was just teasin' you," the man said with a grin. "Want to tell us who she is?"

"So you could try to steal her? I don't think so. You're too handsome for your own good." With a laugh, Mike went out the front door into the lightly snowing, crisp night.

He immediately noticed the sports car pulled up in front of the Sheriff's Office. It was low-slung, expensive—and totally useless in Wyoming weather. A man got out of it and looked at Mike.

"Excuse me. Is this the Sheriff's Office?"

Mike turned and looked at the bold black lettering above the door that said Sheriff's Office. Obviously this man was a belt-and-suspenders type.

"Yes, it is. May I help you?"

"No, I'd rather talk to the sheriff."

Mike smiled. "I am the sheriff. Mike Davis," he said, sticking out his hand.

"Oh. How fortunate to run into you. I'm looking for someone."

"Anyone in particular?"

"Well, yes, actually. A doctor, Dr. Randall."

Mike froze. This man had to be from Caroline's past. Could he be the infamous Don?

"And you would be…?"

"Dr. Donald Scott."

So his hunch was right. Don didn't move to shake his hand, and Mike dropped his.

"Have you checked at the clinic?"

"Yes. They refused to give me any information." His irritation showed through.

Mike didn't want to help him. But he had to know if Caroline meant what she'd said about being over Don. "I can help you. I'll show you where she lives."

"Well, thank you very much. I was afraid no one would tell me anything. I am a friend of hers, not a stalker," he added with a laugh.

"I'm not worried," Mike assured him with a hard smile. "If she wants you gone, I'll make certain it happens."

The man actually took a step back. "Shall I follow you in my car?"

"Up to you. I'm walking. It's close."

Don closed his car door and stepped up on the sidewalk. "Lead the way."

Mike strolled forward, feeling the doctor's presence behind him. He didn't like turning his back on the man, so he stepped to the side and asked, "How long have you known Dr. Randall?"

"We went to med school together in Chicago. Ever been to Chicago? It's a wonderful city."

"Yeah, I've been there."

"Really? I didn't think people this far in the middle of nowhere would've traveled much. I bet Caroline is going crazy here."

"Haven't seen any signs of it."

"You probably don't know her as well as I do."

Mike didn't say anything. He thought it best that he keep quiet before he was tempted to say too much.

CAROLINE COULDN'T BELIEVE how nervous she was. What was wrong with her? It was just Mike.

She laughed at that thought. Just Mike. That was why she'd taken another bubble bath, carefully done her makeup and left her hair down. She'd added her favorite perfume as a special touch.

Waiting in the kitchen was a dish of chicken spaghetti, one of her favorite meals, with tossed salad and green beans. She had rolls ready to go in the oven, some cheese and crackers for a starter, and Red's chocolate cake as dessert.

All of that just for Mike. Her smile grew. She couldn't wait for him to arrive. She wanted to tell him how good she felt now. How his anger had awakened her, rescued her from self-pity.

Where was he? Her watch said two minutes to seven. She'd hoped he'd be early. She did a last-minute check. The fire was crackling in the fireplace. The room was warm and welcoming, tidied up for visitors.

Suddenly she heard footsteps outside and looked at her watch. Of course, she should've known. He was exactly on time. He wasn't about to reveal his feelings by being early.

Taking a deep breath, she headed for the door. But she wasn't going to answer it until he knocked. She definitely had that much self-discipline.

When the knock sounded, she swung open the door, a happy smile on her face.

Until she saw that Mike had brought company. Unwanted company.

MIKE FINALLY SPOKE. "Good evening, Caroline. I was on my way over here when I ran into Dr. Scott looking for you. Said he went to med school with you."

"Yes." She didn't say anything else.

"Caro! Aren't you going to invite me in?" Don asked with a happy smile.

Mike almost burst out laughing. Sensitive the guy was not. Anyone could see Caroline wasn't happy with the man's arrival. At least he hoped that was what was wrong.

Without a word, Caroline moved back so they both could enter. "What are you doing here, Don?" she asked as she closed the door.

Don looked puzzled. He turned to Mike, glaring at him, "Now that we're here, I don't need a chaperon."

"I'm afraid you don't quite get it, Don. I was coming here anyway."

Don looked at Caroline. "You mean you invited the sheriff over? Are you having problems? Is someone bothering you?"

"Not until now," Caroline said coolly.

He still seemed puzzled. Mike found it hard to believe anyone this dense could be a doctor.

"Why are you here?" Caroline asked again.

"I came to see you, Caro. I've missed you."

"Janice isn't keeping you company?"

"She's around, but...she doesn't challenge me. She's not very bright." Don took a step closer.

"Pregnant women frequently don't feel well. Perhaps you should be a little more sympathetic."

"She's supposed to do things for me. After all, I'm the doctor. She's just a nurse."

"I never realized you were such a snob." Caroline turned away and moved to the fire, stretching her hands out as if they were frozen.

Mike's beeper went off. Caroline's sounded just the same, so she checked hers, which was on the mantel.

"It's mine," Mike assured her. "May I use the phone?"

"Of course. In the kitchen."

As soon as Mike stepped through the door, Don hurried to Caroline's side. "Darling, you need to get rid of the local law so we can talk. I made a horrible mistake when I married Janice. I don't even think the baby is mine!"

"Frankly, Don, I don't care. I feel sorry for Janice, of course, but it has nothing to do with me."

"Caroline! How can you say that? We meant so much to each other."

"We were a comfortable habit to each other. I've realized it was all a big mistake. I'm sorry you drove all this way, but I don't want to see you."

Mike walked back into the room.

Caroline immediately transferred her attention to him. "Do you have to go?"

"No. But apparently there's a big snowstorm coming. The weathermen missed it. They thought it would just be a few flakes, but they were wrong. It's set to dump a lot of snow because of the gulf stream combining with a cold front.''

Don laughed. ''Things must be really slow out here if you get excited about a snowstorm. Why don't you go take care of business, so Caro and I can visit?''

''No!'' Caroline quickly said. ''No, Mike, please don't go.''

''Of course not,'' he said calmly, smiling at her.

Don looked outraged. ''Are you seeing this local yokel? For God's sake, Caroline, are you out of your mind?''

''Don't you dare talk about Mike like that. He is ten times the man you are,'' she retorted, glaring at her unwanted guest.

Mike grinned. ''Remember, honey, I can take care of myself.''

Don took a step back, looking anxious. ''I won't fight you!''

Mike simply stared at him, his grin in place.

Just then the phone rang and Caroline went to the kitchen to answer it.

''Dad? Hi. How are you?''

''I'm fine. I wanted to be sure you knew about the snowstorm. Do you want to come out here?''

''Oh, thanks, Dad, but I'd better stay here in case we have any emergencies.''

''Well, I'll call Mike and tell him to—''

''He's here, Dad. We're having dinner together.''

''Oh, good. Does he know about the storm?''

''Yes, he does.''

From the next room she could hear male voices. Apparently Don felt he had to try once more to get rid of the competition. ''You need to go back to your office, Sheriff,'' she heard him say. ''Caro doesn't want you here.''

''I believe she asked me to stay. I didn't hear her asking you to do so.''

''You jerk!'' Don yelled. He seemed to be losing his temper a lot tonight, she thought.

Her dad drew her attention back to their phone conversation. ''I hear voices, Caroline. Is someone there besides Mike?'' Jake asked.

''You'd better talk to Mike about the snowstorm, Dad. I'll get him.''

She leaned around the doorjamb. ''Mike? Could you talk to Dad?'' She waited until he got close and she whispered, ''Don't mention Don.''

As soon as Mike took the phone, Caroline spoke to her ex-boyfriend. ''You have to leave. I have no interest in you or your problems. You're a married man, and you need to go home to your wife.''

''Honey, I'll dump Janice. She's not a problem.''

Caroline ground her teeth. ''Don't you get it, Don? I hate your guts, especially because of the way you treat Janice. I'm not leaving Rawhide. I'm where I want to be.''

''You can't mean that. You'll be bored here. Chicago has so much. Change your mind before it's too late.''

Caroline walked over and opened the front door. ''Get out.''

He appeared to finally get the message. Just as he was about to leave her house, Mike hung up the phone and said, ''Stop!''

''Go!'' Caroline countered.

''Caro, you can't send him away tonight. He won't

get too far before the storm rolls in. Especially in the car he's driving.''

"My car will do fine," Don asserted.

"Look, man, I'd like you to leave as much as Caroline does, but you'll die if you get on the road now."

Caroline grabbed Mike's arm. Whispering, she said, "I want him out of here."

"Where's the nearest hotel?" Don asked stiffly.

"We don't have a hotel in town. Maybe Mrs. Brown has an empty room. She runs a bed-and-breakfast. I'll call her," Mike offered.

He moved to the phone again. Caroline stood there, her arms crossed. She'd finally shut the door because snow was blowing in and the warm air rushing out. But she wasn't going to allow Don to stay with her. If Mike wanted to save him, he'd have to find a place for him.

He hung up thc phone. "Sorry, she's full."

"What a miserable place," Don muttered.

Mike moved to Caroline's side. Leaning close, he said, "I could put him up for the night, but I only have one bed."

Caroline looked at him. "I'll be glad to let you sleep in my guest room. But not him."

"I'll be back in half an hour. And I'll be starving. Okay?"

"Deal," she said with a smile.

"Come on, Don. I've got a place you can stay."

The two men left and Caroline put the casserole in the oven. Maybe her evening wasn't going to be ruined, after all.

Chapter Thirteen

The storm was roaring into town. The snow was coming down harder now, making vision difficult. Mike had his sheepskin coat buttoned all the way and his cowboy hat pulled low. Don was hatless and wearing a light corduroy coat. By the time they reached the Sheriff's Office, the man was shivering uncontrollably.

"This weather is horrible."

"No worse than winters in Chicago," Mike said, staring at the man in surprise.

"You've really been to Chicago?"

Mike shoved him into the building. Then he answered, "I lived in Chicago for over ten years. I've seen blizzards there, too."

"And you choose to live here?"

"I do." He looked to the two deputies on duty. "I'm taking this guy up to my apartment. Let me know if he makes any trouble."

Don acted affronted. "Trouble? I resent that."

"Resent all you want. I'm giving you a place to stay until the storm dies down. I'm going upstairs to pack a few things. Then the place will be yours. Get

him some coffee and keep him entertained,'' Mike
ordered the deputies. ''Anything going on?'' he asked
before he went up the back stairway.

''No, sir. Everything's locked up tight.''

''Okay. I'll be back in a couple of minutes.''

Mike ran up the back stairs and pulled a suitcase
out from under his bed. He was taking some spare
clothes just in case the snow kept blowing. And he
was going to spend the days—and nights—with Caroline.

When he came back down the stairs, he found Don
drumming his fingers on one of the desks, impatiently
waiting.

''The apartment is all clear, Don. Go on up and
make yourself at home. Feel free to eat anything in
the fridge or cupboard.''

''Hey, boss, where you gonna be?'' asked one of
the deputies.

''Beep me if you need me, but there probably
won't be much going on.''

''Say, that reminds me. A car came down the street
about ten minutes ago. Driving way too fast. Spun
out a couple of times. I didn't ticket them, though.''

''That's okay,'' Mike said, perturbed by the care-
lessness. ''They didn't hit anything?''

''I don't think so. They stopped at the clinic. I
thought maybe that's why they hurried, but whoever
it was left something on the doorstep and got back in
the car and left town.''

Mike frowned, chasing back a niggling feeling.
There was that one time back in Chicago.... *Best to
check it out,* he thought. Dialing the number for the

clinic, he waited to see if the phone would be answered. Finally a nurse picked up.

"Someone left a package on the front steps. Make sure it's not human," he ordered after identifying himself. "No, I'll wait."

The two deputies just stared at him.

Within a moment, the nurse was back. "Sheriff Davis," she said in a frantic voice, "it's—it's a baby!"

Damn. This was one time he didn't want to be right. "I'll get Doc Randall and be right there."

"What was it, boss?"

He informed his staff and advised them to be alert. He'd investigate over at the clinic. Then he was out the door, his hat pulled low and a scarf protecting his face.

When he reached Caroline's house, he didn't bother to knock. He shoved the door open and stepped inside.

"It's about time. Dinner is ready," Caroline said with a smile.

What a temptation. He unwrapped the scarf so she could understand him. "Caro, someone left a newborn baby on the front steps of the clinic."

"In this storm?"

"Yeah. One of my men saw a car stop there, but it didn't occur to him that the package left off could hold a baby. You've got to come check the infant out."

She was grabbing her coat before he'd finished.

"You'll need a hat and scarf, too. It's blizzard conditions out there. I'll escort you."

"There's no need. Stay here and eat dinner. I don't want it to go to waste."

"We'll heat it up later," he assured her as he put the casserole in the fridge.

When Caroline had pulled on a wool cap and wrapped a matching scarf around her neck, Mike took her arm and led her out into the storm. They struggled forward, clinging to each other. A distance that took a minute in normal weather took five as they fought the wind and snow.

Caroline fell against the wall when they got inside the clinic. "Thanks for helping me, Mike. It's bad out there."

"Yeah. Give me your things and go see what you can do."

A nurse, Susan, appeared at that moment. "Oh, I'm so glad you're here, Doctor." She led Caroline down the hall.

Mike went out front again to see if he could find any sign of the person who'd abandoned the child. But if there had been anything it was buried in the rapidly piling snow.

He went back inside, craving a cup of coffee. He found a pot in the waiting room. After pouring himself a cup, he wandered down to the nursery. He could see Caroline through the glass. She now had on scrubs and she was bent over a tiny form. The baby was under a heat lamp and he could see it moving, which meant, of course, that it was still alive.

Thank God. Both for the baby and for Caroline. He knew she would be heartbroken if she lost this small patient. For at least half an hour, he watched her care for the newborn. She had no idea he was around; her focus was on her patient.

Watching Caroline with the infant was hypnotic.

She took such pains to be gentle, her voice soothing, almost cooing. Her words were like a lullaby, calming the baby, who'd been through a traumatic ordeal.

Mike had to wrestle himself away from the placid scene. Duty called. Among other places, he contacted social services, notifying them of the abandoned infant and possible charge. They informed him they'd shortly be sending a caseworker to check on the child. Mike thought of the irony of this baby being abandoned so close to Christmas. Then again, he reminded himself, unfortunate events didn't stop just because of the holidays.

He was still deep in thought when he returned to see Caroline sitting in a rocking chair and cuddling the infant against her. She offered a bottle of warm milk, while the two nurses tensely watched. When the baby began to suckle, they all relaxed.

Helen noticed Mike standing there and spoke to Caroline, who looked up and smiled at him. Caroline said something to the nurse and Helen hurried out to him.

"Sheriff? Dr. Randall said for me to bring you the box the baby came in and the note."

"There was a note?"

"Yes, sir."

She handed the box over. Mike found a chair and sat down to examine the objects after he put on latex gloves Helen brought him.

He first read the note. "Please care for my baby. My husband was going to kill her if I didn't give her away. She's a good baby. Her name is Rosa."

The box was lined with an old quilt, and there were several blankets, which had been folded over the infant in an attempt to keep her warm. Mike could feel the love that had gone into preparing the baby for this poignant goodbye. Mike doubted any prints could be lifted, but he did find a long strand of blond hair.

He asked the nurse for a plastic bag for the hair sample. He felt sure the DNA from it would match the baby's, proving the mother was blond. But he doubted he'd be able to find her.

He returned to stare through the glass at Caroline, who kissed the baby's soft cheeks and smiled at her. The woman was obviously falling in love.

When the baby went to sleep, Caroline put her in a bassinet under the heat lamp and came out of the area to talk to Mike.

"She's fine," she said immediately. "And she's so sweet. Did you read the note? Her name is Rosa."

"Yes. There's nothing else to identify her."

"No. She's an orphan. But at least her mother saved her life. It must've been very hard to give her up like this."

"Yeah. Are you ready to go eat?"

"Oh. I'm sorry, Mike, but I can't leave the baby. I need to see her through the night to be sure she's okay. You go ahead. Just help yourself to the food."

"What are you going to eat?"

"I don't know. I'll see what I can find."

"I'll be back with dinner in a few minutes."

He got up and headed for the door.

"Mike, there's no need—" She broke off abruptly because he was out of sight.

Caroline went to her office and sat down behind the desk. Helen knocked on her door. "Susan and I brought dinner. Would you like to share?"

"No thanks, Helen. Mike went to my house to get the dinner I'd made earlier. If he's not back soon, I'll get a pack of cookies from the vending machine."

Helen shook her head. "That's not a proper meal."

"Don't worry. Mike will be back in a few minutes. I may even have enough food for both of you."

"Hmm, what will he be bringing?" Helen asked.

Caroline laughed. "I made chicken spaghetti. And there's a chocolate cake Red baked."

"One of Red's chocolate cakes? Mercy, I hope that man comes back. I once had a piece of a cake Red made. Whooee! I was happy for days."

Caroline grinned. "I know. I even forget what his cakes do to my hips."

"Well, I'm going to be praying the sheriff returns with that dinner you cooked. Hot food sounds so much better than a cold sandwich."

Half an hour later, they heard knocking at the back door. Helen was closest and she opened the door to peep out. Then she swung it wide. "Come in, Sheriff! Can I help you carry something?"

"The cake is on top," Mike said through frozen lips.

"Bless you," Helen said, taking the plate as if it were precious crystal. "This way to the kitchen."

Fifteen minutes later, the four of them gathered around the kitchen table and Caroline dished up the casserole she'd made. She hadn't pictured her special dinner being eaten like this, but she was grateful for the food.

They'd heated it in the microwave and the whole kitchen was redolent with a heavenly aroma. When

Mike took his first bite, Caroline waited for his reaction.

"Caro, this is great! I had no idea you could cook." He reached for another bite.

"Mildred and Red made sure all of us could cook. They said they weren't raising any prima donnas who had to be waited on." She grinned as Mike laughed. The two nurses said they'd write a thank-you note to Red.

Then conversation halted as they all enjoyed the casserole, salad and green beans.

"I haven't eaten anything so good in years," Susan said.

"Just wait, honeychild," Helen said. "When you taste Red's chocolate cake, you'll forget all of this."

Mike raised his eyebrow. "It's that good?"

"It is to me. Have you ever had some?"

"No. I turned it down once."

"Oh, I'd never do that. It's wonderful."

Mike looked at Caroline. "Can you make one of those?"

"No," Caroline said with a rueful grin. "Red keeps that recipe a secret."

"Red's famous for his chocolate cake," Helen added.

Caroline stood up and dispensed with the paper plates they'd used. She put out four clean ones and took a knife to cut the cake. "Okay, I'm cutting big pieces. We all need extra calories to keep warm."

No one objected.

Ten minutes later, the four pieces of cake had disappeared.

"Well, now I understand why Red's cake is famous," Mike said with a sigh. "It's good stuff."

"Oh, yeah," Helen agreed. "It makes working nights worthwhile."

They all heard the weak cry of a baby.

Caroline checked her watch. "She's right on time. Mike, why don't you go to my house? I'm going to be here all night."

She headed for the nursery, leaving Mike to explain to the two nurses. "I have a...boarder staying in my apartment. She offered me her guest room."

"Oh. I see," Helen said. But Mike caught the curious glances between her and Susan.

Mike tried to change the subject. "Say, is Harry awake?"

"He's not supposed to be," Susan answered. "I gave him a sleeping pill."

Mike nodded. "Then I guess I'll go on to bed. Who knows what will happen tomorrow?"

"We know what you mean," Helen assured him.

Mike put on his coat and headed for the door. But on the way, he stopped and watched Caroline giving a bottle to Rosa. He could see the care and devotion she was lavishing on the infant, and he was concerned.

He made his way through the storm to her house, seeing no one else out in the storm. Once he got there, he called his office and praised the deputy for saving a baby's life. Nothing else was going on, the man reported. The visitor had gone up to bed and everything was quiet.

Mike undressed down to his boxers and crawled into Caroline's bed. It wasn't how he'd hoped the evening would end. He'd hoped he could convince her to once again spend the night with him. He wanted to hold her close.

He fell asleep in her bed, but when he woke up the next morning, he was still alone. She'd never come home.

"Dr. Randall?"

Someone was shaking her shoulder. Caroline slowly opened her eyes and raised her head. "What is it, Helen?"

"The baby is awake again. Want me to feed her this time?"

"No. I'll come."

"But you're not getting enough sleep. Why don't you stay in bed and I'll feed her?"

Caroline couldn't quite remember why it was important she feed the baby. Finally she fell back on the hospital bed and nodded. "Okay." Within seconds, she was asleep once more.

When she woke up again, she couldn't tell the time of day by looking out the window, all she could see was white. She rubbed her eyes and then looked at her watch. Ten o'clock? She'd stayed up late to feed the baby. Then she'd lain down for a little while, but Helen was supposed to wake her.

Caroline hurried out of bed and washed her face in the bathroom. She tidied her hair and then set out to find a nurse.

"Helen?" she called as she walked into the nursery. Susan peered around a corner.

"Susan, where's Helen?"

"She's sleeping now," the woman said. "I slept

earlier. We figured we're stuck here until after the storm passes. When we got calls from the nurses due in, saying they couldn't get through, we told them we'd manage until the storm ended.''

"That's very good of you, Susan. But Helen was supposed to wake me up to take the baby's feedings. Why didn't she?''

"She did, Dr. Randall. But she offered to handle it and you agreed and went back to sleep.''

"I see. How's the baby doing?''

"Fine. We're keeping her under the heat lamp, just to be sure. She sleeps well, now that she's being fed regularly.'' Susan looked over her shoulder at their patient. "She's a sweet thing.''

"Yes, she is. I feel so sorry for her mama.'' Caroline ducked her head. "Thanks for working so long.''

"It's okay. Harry's the only other patient, and he's so much better it's hard to keep him in bed.''

Caroline smiled. "How about another piece of cake? We can save a piece for Helen.''

"Ooh, I'd love that. Is there enough for Harry, too?''

"Of course. Has the sheriff called this morning?''

"No, ma'am, but it was pretty late when he went to bed. He may have slept in, too.''

"Yes, I guess so.'' Caroline drew a deep breath. "Well, let's go have breakfast.''

They took the cake into Harry's room and the three of them ate together.

"The sheriff was here last night?'' Harry said.

It was Susan who replied. "Yes. He asked about you, but I told him you were already asleep.''

"I was because you insisted on my taking that sleeping pill. I don't need those anymore."

Susan glanced at Caroline.

"Maybe you're right, Harry," Caroline said. "If we didn't have a storm outside, I'd probably release you today. Obviously you'll have to stay until the storm ends, but I'll take you off the sleeping pills."

"Thank you, Caroline." Harry grinned. "See, Susan? She listens to reason."

"Yes, she does," Mike said from the door. "At least from some people."

"Mike!" Caroline exclaimed. "Has the storm let up?"

"Not really. The weather report says it will pass by tomorrow morning." Mike moved to Caroline's side. "Reckon I could have a bite of that cake, Caro?"

She put her plate down on the bedside table. "I'll go cut you one."

Mike watched her leave, then turned to his deputy. "When are you getting out of this place, Harry?"

"The doc said if it wasn't snowing, she'd let me go today. So I guess I'll be going home tomorrow, after the snow stops."

"Good. How's our newest patient, Susan?"

"She's perfect. She's even gained a little weight." The nurse smiled. "We've all fallen in love with her."

"Yeah. I know." He managed a smile, too, but he was worried about Caroline. He knew how much she wanted a child and how attached she'd already seemed last night.

Caroline came back in and gave him his piece of chocolate cake.

"How's everything at the office?" Harry asked. "Is it quiet?"

"Yes, it is. The guys on duty are staying there until tomorrow. I told them they could use my shower."

"Boy, it'll be nice when they finish that workout room with three showers. Did they get it walled in before the snow came?"

"Yes, they did. It's going pretty fast, there are so many men working on it," Mike assured him.

Harry looked at Caroline. "Caro, your family is really special."

"Yes, they are. But we've been blessed, Harry. It's easier to give when your kids aren't starving."

"I know that should be true," Susan said, "but I've known some wealthy families who never help anyone out. And some poor ones who share everything they have."

Caroline acknowledged her point.

Just then Mike's beeper went off. After pulling it out of his pocket and looking at it, he said, "I've got to call the office. Excuse me."

He used the phone in the waiting room. "Joe, it's Mike. What's up?"

"It's that man who was sleeping upstairs. He got mad when I went up to take a shower. When I got out of the bathroom, he was packed and hauling his suitcase downstairs. He wants to leave."

"He's driving a low-slung sports car. He won't get far, and then he'll freeze to death. Lock him up."

"Sheriff, he's not going to like that."

"I don't really care. I'm not letting him commit suicide today. You can assure him you're just following orders. And tell him I'll personally escort him out of town as soon as I can."

Chapter Fourteen

"You put Don in jail?" Caroline asked in surprise. "Why?"

Mike looked at her, ignoring the others in Harry's room. "Because he was determined to leave. There's no way he'd make it, and I didn't want to have to go haul out his frozen or dead body."

"If he tries to sue you, I'll bear the cost, whatever it is," she offered.

Mike shrugged. "Maybe I could make a case for reckless endangerment. If not, we've got insurance."

"I'd like to see him in jail. Do you give tours?"

"Afraid not. You'll have to entertain yourself some other way."

"Party pooper," Caroline said with a grin. "Okay, I don't really care as long as he leaves town as soon as possible."

"I think he'll be happy to comply."

"Who is this guy?" Harry asked.

Mike said nothing, leaving it up to Caroline to explain.

"He's a jerk I used to know in Chicago. He came to tell me his wife doesn't understand him."

"Eeew," Susan said. "No wonder you want him to go."

"Yes," Caroline agreed. "And she's pregnant."

"Oh, I think you should've let him leave this morning."

"You're being a little bloodthirsty, aren't you?" Harry asked.

"He got her pregnant and married her, but now he wants to have someone on the side? And you don't think that's bad?" Susan demanded.

"He did say he thinks the baby isn't his." Mike looked at Caroline. "What do you think about that?"

Caroline had a surprised look in her eyes. "I never thought about that. I suppose it's possible but—" She stopped, frowning.

"I think we'll just hustle him out of town," Mike said. "I don't think he'll want to come back."

"Well, I hope this storm ends soon. I have more Christmas shopping to do," Susan said with a smile.

At that, Caroline turned to Mike. "I'd almost forgotten. Mike, I need to talk to you," she said, moving toward the door.

He followed her after telling the other two goodbye, and found her leaning against the wall outside the room.

"I was supposed to invite you to Christmas at the ranch. We'd go out Christmas Eve and spend the night. Assuming you're not going to Chicago or Florida to be with your family."

"I'm staying in town, and that sounds wonderful. But Uncle Bill—"

"He'll be invited, too."

"Then I'd love to join the Randalls for Christmas. Especially if Red makes another chocolate cake."

"I'll make a special request," she assured him with a smile.

"Are you coming home tonight?"

"Yes. I need a little more sleep than I got last night."

"Am I still welcome?"

Caroline stared at him. "Why wouldn't you be?"

"Because I don't intend to sleep in the guest room."

Caroline continued to stare at him, but she could think of nothing to say. She wanted him in her bed. But she wasn't sure what the future held. "I—I know."

"I think we need to explore the feelings we have for each other," Mike said.

Caroline nodded. "I had planned for us to talk last night about what's going on, but everything changed when Rosa came into my life. How do you feel about her?"

"Rosa? She's adorable. But that doesn't mean you can keep her. She has parents out there somewhere, Caroline."

"Irresponsible parents. I mean, her mother saved her life, it's true, but if your deputy hadn't seen the car stop at the clinic, the baby would've frozen to death."

"The mother did what she could. I agree that the father shouldn't be given custody, but the woman did her best."

"I wouldn't trust her. I'll go to court and get the legal right to take care of Rosa."

Mike couldn't say anything else. He knew Caroline was thinking that God had brought Rosa to her because the baby needed a mother and she, Caroline, needed a baby. He only hoped she wasn't disappointed.

WHEN CAROLINE LEFT the hospital that evening, around six o'clock, she could tell the storm was easing. It was still snowing, but not as violently. She was glad. But her mind was on the man waiting for her.

She even started planning what she could cook for dinner. Tonight she'd have a chance to talk seriously with Mike. To discuss what they were feeling. And she'd get to sleep in his arms.

When she opened her front door and entered the warmth, she saw a fire burning in the fireplace and smelled a delicious scent in the air. "Mike?"

He stepped out of the kitchen. "Welcome home, Caro. Here, let me help you with that coat." He pulled it off her arms, unwrapped her scarf and then eased the wool cap off her long hair.

"What do I smell? I was going to cook as soon as I got home."

"That seems a little unfair, since I didn't work today." Mike turned back to the kitchen. "Have a seat by the fire and warm up. I'll bring out the hors d'oeuvres."

"How nice. You don't need any help?"

"Nope. I've got it all under control."

She sat down on the sofa and propped her feet on the coffee table, staring at the fire. This was the first chance she'd had all day to sit and relax, and she could feel her eyes slowly begin to close.

"Here we go, my lady," Mike's voice stirred her.

"What is it?" she asked, eyeing the dish he held.

"Nachos. Well, chips and cheese, anyway. I didn't put any jalapeños on them, in case you don't like them."

"How nice." She sat up, removing her feet from the table.

He settled beside her, offering her the plate.

She took one and tasted the warm cheese and chips. "These are good."

"Not exactly haute cuisine, but something I could fix."

"I think it's so nice of you to cook for me." She smiled as she took another chip.

"You're worth the effort. How did your day go?"

"Fine. Rosa is doing so well. It's like she recognizes me. But I don't seem to have the stamina I used to have. I was very tired by evening."

"We'll go to bed early," he promised, his hazel eyes twinkling.

"How sacrificial of you!" she teased.

"That's me. But first I'm going to feed you so you'll have a lot of energy."

"I think I need that," she said with a sigh.

A timer went off and Mike got up. "Want to eat in the kitchen? Or do you want me to bring it in here?"

"Bring it in here. I don't feel like moving."

He returned with two plates, each laden with a juicy steak and a baked potato. Then he went back into the kitchen and brought in hot rolls.

"Oh, Mike, this is wonderful. Exactly what I was hungry for."

They ate silently, enjoying the food. And anticipating what would follow.

Halfway through the meal, Caroline stopped eating. Mike frowned. "You through?"

"Yes. I'm full."

"You haven't eaten all that much. Is it my cooking?"

"Absolutely not. It tasted delicious."

"You used to have a better appetite."

"Mike, you haven't known me that long. And these were big steaks. I'll wrap it up and have it for lunch tomorrow."

"I'll do it. I'll wrap up mine, too. You want to take a shower?"

"Oh, I'd love that. You don't mind?"

"Of course not. I want you to relax."

Caroline thought if she relaxed much more, she'd be asleep on her feet. She put her arms around Mike's neck. "You're wonderful, Mike. Thanks."

In her bedroom, she stripped and tossed her clothes in the laundry hamper. Then she turned on the shower. When the water was hot, she stepped in and let out a big sigh as she felt the heat run down her body. She even washed her hair. Five minutes later, she got out of the shower and slipped into a silk nightgown. Then she combed her long hair and braided it wet.

When she stepped into the room, Mike was sitting on the edge of the bed. He stood and drew a deep breath. "You look fantastic. I'll definitely hurry." He entered the bathroom.

She pulled the covers over her after getting in bed. She'd missed her bed last night. Closing her eyes, she told herself she was just going to rest until Mike came out.

She'd almost fallen asleep when she heard the door open. Slowly she raised her eyelids. Mike hadn't bothered with underwear or pajama bottoms. He had a towel around his waist, and a drop or two of water still clung to his broad chest.

Without hesitation he pulled off the towel and slid into the bed. "You aren't too tired?"

"No. No, I'm not. I've been waiting for a long time, Mike. I want you to hold me."

"I'm willing, lady. For the rest of my life," he whispered, taking her into his arms. He kissed her with a rare combination of passion and gentleness. She loved it.

His callused fingers glided over the silky skin of her shoulders until they reached the strap of her night-gown. He pulled back and looked at her. "This has to go," he said. "I'm ahead of you." As if to under-score his words, he moved against her, and on her thigh she could feel the hard ridge of his arousal.

She drew the slippery fabric over her head and he trapped her hands on her pillow, holding them captive there as he raked his gaze over her breasts.

The hungry look in his eyes was all it took for Caroline to ache for him. She could see how much he wanted her, how much he struggled to hold in his needs.

Pulling her hands free, she reached down and touched him, guided him to the place that would give them both the solace they sought.

She wrapped her legs around him and thanked the

stars that had led her here, back home to Rawhide, to this man. She couldn't think of a better place to be.

THE IRRITATING SOUND of his beeper woke Mike the next morning. He dove out of bed to find it before it woke Caroline. With a frown, he grabbed his jeans and pulled them on. Then he went to the kitchen to call the jail.

"Yeah, it's Mike," he said when one of his deputies answered.

"This guy wants to leave. Can we let him go?"

"Tell him I'm on the way. I'll let him go as soon as I make sure the snowplow is out."

After checking to make sure Caroline was still sleeping, he quietly dressed. He left a note by the pot of coffee he put on so she'd find it when she awoke. Then he went to work.

Don was holding on to the bars and haranguing the deputies when he arrived. Mike walked over to his cell and asked his deputy to open the door. But instead of releasing the man, he walked inside and asked the deputy to lock it again.

"What's going on?" Don asked, a tinge of fear creeping into his voice.

"My men are going to find out how far the snowplow has gotten, so you won't have to drive ten miles an hour to get out of town." Mike sat down on the bunk. "And while we're waiting, you and I are going to have a conversation."

"What about?" he inquired warily.

"How long have you been impotent, Don?"

Mike prided himself on how well he read people—

it was part of his success as a lawman—and he was almost sure he had Don's number.

His suspicion had begun as a niggling thought in his mind last night, and had gnawed at him all day until he could no longer ignore it. The man was so slimy, so weak, that Mike wouldn't put it past him to hide behind Caroline's problem. To get confirmation of his theory, Mike decided to simply accuse Don and gauge his reaction. If it were true, he expected the sniveling doctor to cave right in.

The man seemed to visibly puff up his chest like a threatened bird.

"Hey! I can get it up with the best of them."

"Yeah, but you shoot blanks, right?"

Don looked away. "I don't know what you're talking about."

"Yes, you do. You let Caro think she was the problem. You probably married the nurse because you wanted to convince a few people you could make a baby. But you know the truth. And you let Caro suffer the entire time you were together. Didn't you?" Mike's voice changed, growing hard and threatening.

"I—I may have—she didn't think—what difference did it make? She can't have kids. It was perfect!" He went from helpless to angry in no time.

Mike glared at him. "You bastard! You stupid bastard!" Then he stood up and called to the deputy. "Come unlock the door."

He stepped out of the cell and held the door open. "Get out of my jail. Out of my town. And don't come back here ever again. Do you understand?"

"Why would I ever want to come back? This place is dead!"

Mike said nothing. He just held the door open.

"Has the snowplow—"

"Out!"

Don took one look at Mike's face and chose to do as he was ordered. He hurried out into the cold air. His car had over a foot and a half of snow on it and he tried to clear the windshield.

When he couldn't stand looking at him anymore, Mike opened the door and glared at him. Don gasped. Then he jumped into his car, with only half the snow wiped off the body of it, and backed out of his parking space. He floored the gas, which only caused the tires to spin helplessly.

Finally he managed to pull his car out onto the road, only to fall in behind the slow-moving snowplow.

Mike grinned. The man would be behind the snowplow for the next two hours, at least until he got to Buffalo. Good.

WHEN CAROLINE OPENED her eyes, she knew she was alone. She'd had visions of lingering in bed with Mike. Maybe even repeating their lovemaking, if he was so inclined.

She looked at the clock beside her bed. It was 10:00 a.m. The late hour didn't upset her. After all, she'd pulled extra duty during the snowstorm, while Jon had been at home. He could hold down the fort until she got to the clinic.

She was still in bed when the phone rang five minutes later. "Hello?"

"How are you, Caro?"

She loved the sound of Mike's voice, deep and

smooth. "I'm doing fine, Mike. I slept in this morning and I feel good."

"Great. I was worried about you, you were so tired last night."

"Oh, it was just missing too much sleep the night before. I'm no spring chicken, you know."

"Need me to come help you get up?" he asked. "Or serve you breakfast in bed?"

"Mmm, it sounds tempting, but I'd better get to the clinic."

"Okay. How about I buy you dinner at the café tonight?"

"I'll treat you. After all, you cooked last night."

"I wouldn't turn down an offer like that."

"At six?"

"Perfect."

She hung up the phone and got ready for her day. Suddenly it seemed a much better one, knowing that Mike would be waiting for her.

When she reached the clinic, the first thing she did was check on Rosa. The baby turned her head toward Caroline when she heard her voice. Caroline leaned over and kissed her cheek. "That's your reward for being so smart, little girl," she whispered.

"Hey, Caro, glad to see you made it in," Jon teased when he caught up with her in the hall.

She put her hands on her hips in a mock-defiant stance. "Don't start with me, Jon Wilson. I was here throughout the storm while you were at home with your family."

Jon smiled. "I know. That's why I wanted to urge you to take some time off."

"Thanks, but no. I just slept late this morning. I

seem to have less energy these days. But I'm okay now."

"Want me to give you a once-over?"

"No, thanks. I may start taking a multivitamin, though." She knew Jon was studying her, and she shrugged as she grinned. "I'm not your patient, Jon."

"I don't know who else's you'd be."

"I've just come through a period of stress. I'll feel more energetic now."

"Okay. Did you finish your Christmas shopping this past weekend?"

"Most of it. I'm glad we're drawing names for Christmas."

"Yeah. Otherwise, we'd have to start shopping in June."

Caroline laughed. "Right, because you do so much of the shopping."

She headed to her office, but Jon called, "I do some!"

Waving to him, she entered her office. The truth was she'd been a little worried about her exhaustion last night. But this morning she was doing fine.

She'd packed her leftover dinner from last night for her lunch today. Steak would provide the protein her body needed. But a couple of hours after lunch, she was feeling tired again.

Leaving the clinic at four o'clock, she crawled into bed and set the alarm clock for a quarter to six. As soon as her head hit the pillow, she fell asleep.

When the alarm went off, she had to force herself out of bed. She studied her face in the bathroom mirror. No sign of flu or virus. But she promised her reflection that she'd let Jon give her a checkup if she didn't feel better soon. Shrugging off any concern for now, she redid her hair and then headed to the café.

Mike was standing at the door of the restaurant, waiting for her.

"Am I late?" she asked.

"Nope. I just missed you."

She smiled, pleased with his response. "I'm glad you asked me. It gave me something to look forward to all day."

He bent over and kissed her lips.

"Mike! Everyone will see us."

"Good. I don't want any of the guys thinking you're available."

"Would you be jealous?" she asked with a coy grin.

"Damn right!"

He took her hand and led her to a corner table in the rear of the café. "We won't be noticed as much back here."

Caroline found those words amusing, especially since numerous people came by their table to speak to them.

When Harry stopped by, Caroline wanted to know how he was doing. He sat down at the table to answer her, and Mike glared at him. Harry jumped up, a contrite look on his face. "Sorry, boss." He left the café.

"Mike Davis! What's wrong with you?" Caroline admonished. "I needed to see how he's doing."

"He's doing fine."

"I didn't think you were a doctor!"

"And I didn't ask you here to share you with a lot of other men, Caroline." He leaned in close to her. "I want you all to myself."

Chapter Fifteen

Mike spent every free minute with Caroline over the next few days—and nights. As much as he relished their time together, he became increasingly concerned about her lack of stamina. He'd warned her that she was overdoing it, trying to finish her Christmas shopping in addition to work. He'd even noticed she couldn't run as long as he did on their morning jogs.

When he expressed concern, she dismissed it. Mike encouraged her to take a nap in the afternoon, to which she didn't object. It was already becoming part of her routine, she said.

Unbeknownst to Caroline, Mike had called Jon the day after the snowstorm. He'd asked Jon to keep an eye on her and make sure she didn't get too tired.

"Is something wrong?" Jon asked.

"I'm not sure. But her energy level is different than it was when she first came back. I'm just a little worried."

"I didn't know it was the sheriff's business to keep an eye on everyone's health. You're going to be one busy man."

Mike growled, "You know it's personal. Don't give me any lip," he added with a grin.

"I know, but I wasn't sure you knew."

"Most men notice when they've been struck by lightning," Mike said. "But I promised myself I'd go slow."

"I think Jake would prefer that you take her by storm," Jon said with a laugh.

"You think he'll approve?"

"Are you kidding? I heard you were his personal choice for his only son-in-law."

"I'd like to think that. But it's Caroline's choice that matters to me most."

"She seems interested."

"Being interested is a long way from being committed."

"It's hard to commit if you haven't been asked," Jon stated. "My wife pointed that out to me last night when we were discussing you and Caroline."

"You were discussing us?" Mike asked in surprise.

"Hell, Mike, half the town is talking about the two of you. Every time you appear in public, every night you spend at Caro's house, every smile she gives you—it's all discussed. We can't wait until there's another Randall party."

"I had no idea I was holding up a celebration." He cleared his throat. "Just keep an eye on Caro."

"Will do. Are you coming to the ranch for Christmas?"

"Yes, I am."

"Good. See you then."

When Mike met Caroline at the café again for dinner a couple of nights later, he discovered she had another problem. "What's wrong?" he asked as she frowned.

"Oh. I drew Casey's name for Christmas. I've got everyone else's presents, but I haven't been able to come up with anything good for him, and tomorrow's Christmas Eve."

"I have something you can give him."

"What?"

"Michael Jordan had a big picture book out a few years ago. I have an autographed copy. I think Casey would love it."

"Let me buy it from you," she said eagerly.

"It's not necessary to pay me for it. Every time I move I think about getting rid of it because it's so heavy. I'll be glad to see it find a new home."

"And what do you want Santa to bring you for Christmas?" Caroline asked.

"I'm not telling."

"Why not?"

He just smiled.

"Well, I've bought you one present, but I'd like to get you something else."

Mike smiled again. He had a present for Caroline, too, but he wasn't sure she'd accept it. He'd promised to go slow, but he was finding it difficult to hold back.

He reached across the table and caught her hand. "Did you get tired today?"

She looked away. Finally she glanced at him. "I made it fine…but I took a nap after lunch. Jon saw a couple of patients for me. I had to apologize when I woke up, but he didn't seem to mind. Then I took his last two patients so he could go home early."

"That was nice of you. Then the vitamins aren't making a difference?"

"It's too early to tell. They have to have time to build up. Christmas will give me a chance to catch up. Jon says the clinic is open only for emergencies. I intend to sleep late every day."

Mike gave her a half smile. "Want some company?"

She squeezed his hand. "Oh, yes. By the way, when are Bill and Margie going to get married?"

"I think New Year's Eve. Bill said he wanted to start the new year off as a married man."

The waitress picked up their empty plates. "How about dessert?"

"I shouldn't," Caroline said.

"But you will. She'll have a slice of coconut pie, and so will I," Mike stated with a smile.

"Mike, you're going to get me fat."

"I find that hard to believe, since you've been jogging with me in the mornings. I hear we're entertaining the entire town. They're all getting up early to see if you run with me."

Caroline looked shocked. "Really? They're that interested in my exercise program?"

"No, honey, they're that interested in your private life."

"I guess that means Dad knows that we run together?"

Mike couldn't hold back a chuckle. "I suspect he knows a lot more than that."

"Oh. Has he said something to you?"

"No, not yet. He just gives me a stern look when they come to build the workout room."

"If Dad says something to you, just tell me."

"Why? I think that's his right. You're his little girl."

"Silly me. I thought I was an adult."

Mike grinned. "You are an adult. A very beautiful adult. But you'll always be your dad's little girl."

"It's a good thing he didn't know Don was in town," Caroline said with a sigh.

"He did."

"He did? But why—?"

"I told him I'd get rid of the man."

"Oh."

The waitress brought their slices of pie. Caroline picked up her fork. "I'm glad you talked me into this, even if it is a thousand calories."

Mike smiled and said nothing.

"We'll go out to the ranch about two o'clock tomorrow. Is that okay with you?"

"I'm looking forward to spending Christmas with your family," he said.

"Me, too. I'm thankful I can now appreciate them and be glad I came home."

Once they'd finished their dessert, Mike went to his apartment and found the book with Michael Jordan's autograph. He took it to Caroline's and she wrapped it up after admiring it. "How did you get it autographed?"

"I used to work security at the Bulls games. I brought the book with me one evening and asked him to sign it. He did. He's a considerate man."

"Once I tell Casey where I got it, he'll think you walk on water. He already thinks you're hot stuff." So did she, but in a different way.

"Do you need any help wrapping presents?" she asked.

"No, thank you. The general store wraps anything you buy for Christmas." He'd bought hospitality gifts for the Randalls and several things for Caroline, other than the big present he'd bought her. "I'll have everything ready by two tomorrow."

He stood up. Caroline gave him a surprised look. "Aren't you staying the night?"

"I've got to do some things before I leave tomorrow, so I'd better go home this evening."

"Oh, of course," she agreed readily.

He leaned over and kissed her goodbye. Then he left.

Caroline sat on the floor where she'd been wrapping, staring into the fire. She missed him so much when he didn't stay with her. She felt stronger, more at peace with everything when she was with Mike.

What if he didn't feel the same? What if he didn't want to marry a woman who was childless? She might get to adopt Rosa, but it was also possible the baby's parents would show up. She loved the little girl, but she was trying not to get too involved just yet.

Besides, as tired as she was, Caroline couldn't handle a baby and her work, too.

But most of all, she couldn't do without Mike. A scary thought.

She was comfortable back in Rawhide now. She realized she'd been feeling sorry for herself all those years. But taking the last step—agreeing to marry a man who said it was okay to not have kids and believing him—was difficult.

She wanted to. God, how she wanted to. She didn't want to give up Mike. She'd let herself fall for him, hard. Her day improved drastically when she knew Mike would be in it. In his presence, she felt smarter, brighter, prettier. Without him, the hours seemed to blur.

She couldn't imagine a lifetime without him in it.

THE NEXT AFTERNOON at exactly two o'clock, Mike pulled up in his SUV, got out and knocked on her door. Caroline swung it open, and he swept her up in his arms and kissed her. "I've missed you," he whispered.

"Me, too," she replied fervently.

"I don't suppose we'll share a room at your folks' ranch?"

"Not likely," she said. "You'll be confined to the bachelor pad. That's what they call the boys' bunkhouse."

"Not exactly what I had in mind," Mike said with a laugh.

"Me, neither," she assured him. "I haven't ever wished for Christmas to be over, until now."

"And you're going to take some time off after Christmas, so you can rest up, aren't you?"

"Yes, worrywart. I'll get all rested up."

"Good." He kissed her again. "I guess that will have to do me for a while."

He loaded all the gifts she had wrapped, and put her suitcase next to his. Then they drove out to the ranch. They talked the whole way there, both of them eager to share bits and pieces of their job experiences, stories of the townsfolk.

"I got a Christmas card from Tracey Long," Caroline said. He could hear the excitement in her voice. "You remember her?"

Mike recalled Caroline's high school friend who'd been abused by her husband. "Of course. She hear from her no-good husband?"

"No, thank God. But she and the kids are all settled in Denver now with her parents. The girls love it there."

"A happy ending." Though he kept his eyes on the road, he reached out and squeezed Caroline's hand. "I'm glad for you. But I wish I could predict the same for Holly Gambil."

"Yeah," Caroline said. "I checked on her father and he told me Nick helped them get a good attorney."

"They're going to need one. From what I hear, the trial date's not that far away." Mike shook his head. He never could understand why people resorted to violence, no matter how emotional their situation. The image of a distraught young Holly still stayed in his mind. "I hope it turns out okay for her. She's going to need lots of help getting her life back. And Mr. and Mrs. Gambil, too."

In his profession—and in Caroline's—there wasn't always a happy ending. He guessed that was why he felt elated when it did work out for someone. And baby Rosa? he wondered. How would the story end for her?

He never got the chance to consider it, as they'd arrived at the Randall ranch.

"Your dad must have his own snowplow," Mike

said, noticing how clean the drive was, with a ridge of snow down each side.

"Oh, yes, he has the kind that attaches to the tractors. He used to let me ride with him when I was a little girl. I loved watching the snow spiral up into the air before falling on the side of the road."

"That's a great memory," Mike said.

He could feel Caroline looking at him. "You never talk about your childhood, Mike. Is it too painful?"

"Nah." He shrugged. "It was what it was. Life was hard for my mom, being all alone with the three of us. She worked a lot and we kind of got by. At least we had Uncle Bill. And my sisters took great care of me. A benefit of being the youngest, I guess. But my mother...well, she did the best she could." Mike glanced at Caroline. "It wasn't all bad, you know. We did have some fun times. My sisters and I could really get my mother going." He broke out in a grin at the memories.

"I called them all this morning to wish them a Merry Christmas," he continued. "My mom said it was eighty-one degrees in Florida, can you believe it?"

"It must be hard not being together at the holidays," Caroline said. She rubbed his arm gently. "You know, lately it seems the more people I talk to, the more I realize how much I have to be grateful for."

"You sure do." At the turn in the driveway, he said, "Will Sarah and Nick be here?"

Caroline stared at him, not understanding the change of subject. "Well, yes, I think so. Why?"

"No reason. I just remembered seeing Sarah at the

store the other day. She wanted to give me a discount because we got rid of their thieves. I told her to offer it to Harry.''

''That was nice of you.''

Mike shrugged his shoulders.

Then, since they were on the driveway, not the county road, he pulled to a stop.

''What are you doing? Is something wrong?''

Mike took a deep breath. ''Yeah. I was going to wait until tomorrow, but I can't. I brought you this present.'' He pulled a small box out of his coat pocket.

''Don't you want to wait until we open presents in the morning?''

''Nope. If you won't accept it, I'd rather you turn me down in private.''

He noticed her breathing hitch, and she took the box in shaking fingers. ''I—I...what is it?''

''You're supposed to open it.''

He was as nervous as she was, and had to fight the urge to tear the paper off the small package. When she finally pulled it off, he took a deep breath. ''Okay. Now you can open the box.''

She eased it open. Inside was a dark green, smaller box, a jewelry box. Slowly she pried it open and gasped. Then she stared at him.

For the first time he had a hard time reading someone. ''Well? Do you like it?''

''Oh, mercy, Mike! It's stunning!''

''Sarah sold it to me. But will you accept it?''

''What finger should I wear it on?''

He looked at her as if she were crazy. ''Lady, that's an engagement ring. And it means a short engagement. I love you so much. I want to take care of you, be there for you, build a life with you.''

Tears glistened in her eyes. ''Even if there are no children?''

''Hell, yes! Haven't I convinced you of that?''

''Yes! I just had to ask one more time. Mike, I love *you* so much.''

He gave her a deep kiss, sealing their promise to each other. In fact, it was so powerful, they might have made love right there on the side of the road, if a car hadn't passed them, honking as it went by.

Mike muttered under his breath and helped Caroline sit up. ''Damn, it's Jon. He would just happen by. Here, put the ring on. Sarah said she had your size on record.''

The ring slid onto Caroline's third finger, fitting perfectly.

''My goodness, look how it sparkles, Mike. It must be at least three carats!''

''Four! I wanted you to have a ring you'd be proud of.''

''But, Mike, it must've cost a lot!''

He grinned. ''That's an understatement,'' he muttered.

''But—''

He kissed her again. ''It was my decision. And I like the way it looks on your hand. All I want is for you to want to wear it.''

''Oh, yes I do!''

When they reached the house, Jon and Tori had already gone inside. Mike and Caroline greeted the family, but said nothing about their engagement. Then she asked Red for a cup of hot tea and went out to the kitchen with the women.

It took several minutes for someone to notice the diamond on her finger. Then Mike heard Elizabeth scream, "Caroline, your ring!"

Caroline must have been swamped by all the women, judging from the sounds in the kitchen.

Jake, in the living room with the other men, looked up when he heard the commotion. Like everyone else, he started toward the door, but Mike put a hand on his arm. "Jake, could you wait a moment?"

"You know what's going on?"

Mike nodded. When the others left the room, he said, "I asked Caroline to marry me...and I gave her a ring. I hope you and B.J. don't mind."

"Mind? Hell, no, son. Welcome to the family!" He shook Mike's hand and then hugged him.

"Thanks, Jake," Mike said, a little startled by the man's exuberant reaction.

Suddenly, Jake stepped back. "Did she talk to you about...about children?"

"Yes, sir. If she can't have babies but wants children, we'll find a way. However, I discovered that Don was impotent."

"That bastard!"

"My words exactly," Mike told him. "But he's gone now and he won't be coming back. I scared him away."

Jake clapped him on the shoulder. "Thatta boy! Good job!" He grabbed Mike's arm and started in the direction of the kitchen. "Let's go see what kind of a ring you bought my little girl."

When they entered the crowded kitchen another

eruption occurred. Everyone wanted to welcome Mike into the family and shake his hand. B.J. hugged him, as did all the ladies. And they all raved about the ring.

"Where did you find it?" B.J. asked.

"Ask Sarah. She said she had some private stock for special customers," Mike said, nodding toward the woman.

Nick stepped up next to Jake. "My wife has exquisite taste."

Jake reached his daughter and asked to see her ring. She held out her hand, watching his eyes. He stared at the diamond on her finger, then turned and looked at Mike. "Are you trying to start an uprising, Mike? All the ladies are going to want big rings. Mercy, you must've spent a wad."

Mike grinned. "Caroline is a special lady. I didn't want her to be ashamed of my ring."

"You got that accomplished," muttered Pete, scratching the back of his neck.

Janie put her arm around her husband's waist. "Don't worry, honey. I have something better than Caro's ring."

"You do? What's that?"

"Almost thirty years with you."

The kitchen seemed to turn into a love fest, with wives reassuring their husbands.

"Gol-darn it! Get out of my kitchen with all this lovey-dovey stuff," Red yelled. "I have work to do!"

"I could use some help unloading my SUV. You won't believe how many presents Caroline brought with her." Mike headed out to his car and some of the men followed him. They all loaded up with presents and returned to the big living room used for family gatherings.

Mike stood at the entrance, staring at the huge tree. "How did you get that tree in here? It's beautiful."

"Yeah," Casey said at his side. "It takes us a long time to decorate it. Tonight we'll sing Christmas carols around it. And then Jake will read 'Twas the Night Before Christmas' to all the little kids before they go up to bed."

"That sounds terrific," Mike said.

"And then the parents play Santa Claus," Casey continued. "The rest of us watch and drink eggnog."

"And how early does Christmas start in the morning?"

"There's a rule. No one goes downstairs until the sun has risen. Then it's up to us, but no one wants to miss Christmas morning. Besides, we get to open presents."

No matter what was under that tree in the morning, Mike knew he'd already gotten the best gift.

Chapter Sixteen

Mike enjoyed Christmas Eve, which followed Casey's description. The small children were adorable as they listened to Jake read the story in his deep voice. Some of them sat at his feet. Others stayed in their mothers' laps.

Mike sat with his arm around Caroline. She was relaxed, leaning against him, whispering occasionally. He couldn't imagine being more content. After the story, Anna led everyone in Christmas songs. The voices blended amazingly well. By the time it was all over Mike had to admit he'd never spent such a wonderful Christmas.

A sleepy Caroline kissed him good-night and went up to bed shortly after ten. Mike wanted to go up with her, but, as she'd predicted, he was led to the bachelor pad by Casey. There he found all the unmarried men, even his uncle. They were talking about a variety of subjects including the price of Caroline's ring. But no one asked.

Mike was going to turn in when his beeper went off. After checking it, he asked Casey to lead him to a phone. He used the one in the bunkhouse to call his office.

"What's up?"

"Sheriff, I'm sorry, but we've got this hysterical lady wantin' to see her baby and fearin' her husband will come. We don't know what to do."

"She's the woman who left the infant at the clinic?"

"She says she is, but the nurses wouldn't let her see her baby and she's hysterical."

"Okay, Gary, I'll be right there."

He told Casey he had to go back to town. Casey said his bunk was closest to the door. "Just knock and I'll let you in," he offered.

All the way back to town, Mike worried about what was going to happen. How it would affect his engagement to Caroline.

He'd known all along that she was growing too attached to the baby. He'd watched the two together and had marveled at Caroline's gentle touch, at Rosa's soft coos when she was being held. And he'd known trouble was brewing. He'd told Caroline it was only a matter of days before social services came and took control of the baby—Rosa was getting healthy enough to leave the clinic—but he doubted she listened to him.

Mike raked a hand through his hair. If Rosa was reunited with her mother, Caroline would be devastated. Would she blame him? Would she give him back his ring and end their relationship?

Questions whirred in his head as he pulled up at the clinic. Alice, the nurse on duty that night, explained that the woman had come in and asked for her baby back. When they'd told her no, she'd tried to get past them. Alice had fought her while the other nurse called the Sheriff's Office.

"Your officers were wonderful, Sheriff Davis. They got her out of here."

"Good. I'm going to talk to her."

"Will she get Rosa?"

Mike patted her shoulder. "I don't know. It's not my decision."

When he got to the office, he heard sobbing as soon as he opened the door. The woman was in the first cell, crying her heart out. The two deputies were standing around looking very uneasy.

"Open the cell," Mike ordered, "and don't lock it again."

The woman, who had long blond hair, never looked up. Mike sat down beside her and touched her shoulder. "Ma'am, I'm the sheriff, Mike Davis. What's your name?"

She glanced at him, and he saw that her face was a mess—her eyes swollen, one of them black, with a bruise on her opposite cheekbone.

"Gary, get me some tissue," he called to his deputy. "Ma'am, did my men hurt you like this?" He gestured to her eye.

"Oh, n-no. That was m-my husband."

"Is he here?"

"N-no. I ran away and—and I hitched a ride with a truck driver."

"And your name?"

"Mary Hudson."

"And your husband's name?"

She shook her head and covered her face.

"Mrs. Hudson, I need to know your husband's name and his location."

"I left him in Salt Lake City. His name is…is Perry Goodson."

"You're not really married to him?"

She covered her face again and sobbed some more.

"Okay, I need some more information. Why do you think your baby is in our clinic?"

"B-because I left her on the steps. If I hadn't, that bastard was going to kill her. He said he couldn't get enough sleep when she cried."

"And did you name your baby?"

"Yes! Yes, I named her Rosa because she was as pretty as a rose. My mom was named Rose. I wanted her to have her own name, so I change it to Rosa."

He asked her several more questions. Then he said, "If I take you to see your baby, will you accept the fact that you can't take her out of the clinic tonight?"

She grabbed his hand. "I can see her? She's all right?"

"Yes. I understand she's putting on weight and seems happy. But you're going to have to appear before a judge and prove that you can take care of your baby. That you won't abandon her again."

"I won't! I promise! But I can't afford a lawyer or anything. I'll never get her back. Please help me!"

"The main thing you have to do is calm down. You can't see Rosa like this."

"I—I will," she said, hiccuping a little.

"Do you have a coat?"

"I have a sweater," she said, looking wildly around her.

Gary stepped forward and held her sweater out for her to slip her arms into the sleeves.

Mike handed his keys to Gary. "Run upstairs. I have a couple of coats in my closet. Bring one of them down."

Mary looked confused. "I'm fine with my sweater."

"It's cold outside, ma'am. Where did you come from?"

"Salt Lake City."

"No, I mean where's your family?"

"My dad lives in Kentucky. My mom's dead. I— I ran away with Perry. Dad told me not to come back. I knew I'd made a mistake, but I didn't have anywhere to go. Then I got pregnant and I hoped Perry would like our baby."

Gary came down with a heavy jacket and held it out for Mary.

Mike took her outside to his SUV. He helped her in and circled the vehicle to drive her to the clinic.

Once they got there, Mary seemed afraid. "I don't think they'll let me in."

"Yes, they will. I'll make sure of it."

Mike led her into the clinic and rang the bell for assistance.

The two nurses came together, their eyes wide and wary. "Sheriff," Alice said in greeting.

"Ladies, this is Mary Hudson. She left her baby on the front steps about a week ago because the father threatened to kill her. She understands that she can't take the baby away, but she'd like to hold her and see if she's all right."

"Are you sure she won't hurt her?" Alice asked.

"No!" Mary protested. "I'd never do that. I promise I just want to—to hold her."

The pain in her eyes, the hunger to see her child, convinced the nurses more than Mike's words.

The four of them went down the hall to the nursery. Mary started trembling when she saw the baby sleeping in a bassinet.

Alice put an arm around the woman. "Here, come sit in the rocker. She should be wanting her bottle anytime now. You can feed her."

Mary's eyes lit up with joy. Alice helped her remove Mike's jacket, then the woman sank down in the rocker and stared at her baby, tears running down her face.

Mike leaned against the wall, waiting.

When the baby began stirring, Mary watched her child in awe. Alice picked the baby up and handed her to her mother.

Mike was afraid Rosa would let out a yell, but the baby just latched on to the bottle the nurse had given Mary. When she finished feeding, the nurses showed Mary how to burp her.

Once that was done, exhaustion took effect on the weary mother.

"Come on, Mary." Mike picked up his coat and helped her put it on.

She turned to the nurses and thanked them for taking care of her baby.

"Where are you taking her?" Alice asked.

"I'm going to drive her back to the jail."

"We can keep her here. She might need some attention to that bruise."

"Don't worry," Mike said, realizing he was going

to have another fight on his hands if he didn't convince the nurses he was going to help Mary. "I'm going to put her in my apartment for the night. Tomorrow I'll see what I can do for her. But first she needs to sleep."

"But where will you sleep?"

"I'm spending the night at the Randalls' ranch."

"Will she be able to keep her baby?"

"I don't know. I'm going to ask Nick Randall to help her."

"Good." Alice turned to comfort the mother. "Don't worry, Mary. You'll be okay."

By the time he got the woman back to the Sheriff's Office, she was almost asleep. Mike left her with Gary while he went upstairs and straightened up a little. He found a T-shirt she could sleep in. That was the best he could offer. Then he called down for Gary to bring her up. Mike showed her the bathroom, offered the T-shirt and told her someone would give her breakfast when she woke up.

"Thank you so much," she whispered, obviously overwhelmed.

The two men went down the stairs. Gary muttered, "The man who beat her should be in jail."

Mike nodded in agreement. "Will you keep an eye on her? When she wakes up, take her to breakfast at the café. You can even escort her to see Rosa again. Tell her she'll have to spend the night in my apartment again tomorrow night. Then she'll see Nick Randall to find out what she has to do to get her baby back."

"Sure, boss. Listen, she's a little thinner than my

sister, but I'm sure my sister can give her a few clothes. That might make her feel better.''

"That's very thoughtful of you, Gary, if you think your sister won't mind. After all, tomorrow is Christmas.''

"Couldn't be a better time to give.''

"Good point. I'll be back tomorrow afternoon to see how she's doing.''

"Yes, sir.''

Mike felt sorry for the woman. She seemed so young, so lost. He believed he had to help her.

But what would it do to Caroline? He'd do anything he could for her, because more than anything in the world, he wanted her to be happy. But he couldn't take Rosa from her mother. He had to do his job.

He drove back out to the ranch, feeling like a fraud accepting Jake's warm hospitality while bringing sadness to his daughter. Mike remembered how Jake had welcomed him into the family. That could change, come dawn.

Rapping on the bunkhouse door, Mike waited for a sleepy Casey to open up.

"Come on in. You won't get much sleep if you plan to get up early,'' Casey whispered.

"Yeah, I know. But wake me at sunup anyway, okay?''

"Sure,'' Casey agreed, and yawned.

Mike went to the small room he'd been given and shed his clothes, sliding under the covers. But instead of sleeping, he tossed and turned, fearing the reality of dawn.

CAROLINE HEARD the stirring of the children early the next morning. She thought about staying in bed, but she knew Mike would be waiting for her. She held up her finger and stared at her beautiful ring. He'd certainly surprised her. She knew he wanted to be with her, but she hadn't been sure he wanted anything permanent.

A month ago she'd been in Chicago, hiding out from her family, from her life, thinking herself less a woman, less a potential wife because of her so-called deficiency. Then she'd come to Rawhide and found Mike Davis—and everything had changed.

She thought of little Zach and his mother and the lesson she'd learned from them. Then she thought of Mike and how, thanks to him, she'd learned how much she had to offer. She hugged herself at her luck in finding such a man as Mike.

A knock on her door had her hoping it was him. When she opened it, however, Davy stood there.

"Aunt Caroline? Are you going to come down? Daddy said to come ask you."

The boy's excitement was contagious. "Yes, I am. Let me get my robe and I'll come down with you." She put on a warm robe and slippers and stepped out of her room.

Davy was waiting for her. "Come on, Aunt Caroline. Daddy said we should go to the kitchen first."

She could smell the coffee halfway down the stairs, and picked up speed. Knowing Mike would head for a cup of coffee, she hurried to the kitchen.

He wasn't there.

"Have you seen Mike?" she asked Red and Mildred.

They both shook their heads. Then Red said, "We

heard someone drive off last night. His SUV is out there now, but he may have had a call and not gotten much sleep.''

Caroline was just heading to the bunkhouse to find him when he came in the door with Casey.

''Mike! Are you okay?''

He gave her a haggard smile. ''Fine. But I didn't get much sleep.''

Caroline's heart fell. ''Were you having second thoughts?'' she asked softly.

He pulled her into his arms. ''Never, sweetheart.''

She relaxed against him. ''I would've stayed in bed this morning if you'd been with me.''

His smile brightened. ''I wish I had been.''

''Come on, sit down, and I'll get you some coffee.''

Along with coffee, she brought him a warm cinnamon roll. He drank some coffee first, but once he tasted the cinnamon roll, he finished it before he went back to the coffee. ''Man, that was great. Can you make those, Caro?''

''That's another secret recipe of Red's,'' she told him ruefully.

''Maybe for a wedding present Red will—'' Mike suddenly stopped as the phone rang.

Standing next to it, Caroline picked it up. ''Merry Christmas to you, too,'' she said when the deputy greeted her.

''I'm sorry to bother you all on Christmas, Ms. Randall, but I need to speak to Mike about the baby's mother.''

Caroline felt her chest tighten, her pulse pound. It suddenly became hard to breathe. ''Excuse me?''

"Little Rosa," the deputy clarified. "Didn't Mike tell you? Her mother showed up last night to take her child."

Caroline held back the tears that stung her eyes. She turned to look at Mike.

The man she loved looked like a criminal caught in the act.

"CARO—"

"Why, Mike? Why didn't you tell me?"

He took her hand and led her to the dining room, a silent, empty space where they wouldn't be disturbed.

"I wanted to tell you, Caro. But I was going to wait until after Christmas." He raked a hand through his hair. "Dammit, Caroline, I was afraid."

"Afraid of what, Mike?" She held herself so stiffly, he was sure she'd snap.

"Afraid you'd…change your mind. About us." At the questioning look in her eyes, he continued. "She wants her baby back—and I'm going to help her."

Caroline closed her eyes and turned away. After a few silent moments she faced him again, her face contorted with emotion. "And that's it? She just asks and we hand that fragile child to her?"

Mike heard the rising mixture of temper and tears. "Of course that's not how it is. But I believe I should help her. I'm going to ask Nick to provide her legal aid. One of my deputies is getting her clothes. She has nothing, but she loves her baby more than life itself. The man beat her, but she got away and hitchhiked back to Rawhide."

"And how will she take care of her baby? Does

she have any resources? Any way of supporting herself and her child?''

Mike shook his head. ''No, but—''

''And what about what I can offer her? A stable, safe, secure life.''

As much as it hurt him, Mike had to say it. ''It's not about that, Caroline. She's the baby's mother. Look, if you want to fight her, you go ahead. But I don't think that's the way to proceed.''

''I'd hoped—'' She broke off and bit her bottom lip. As if a dam opened, the tears she'd fought off so valiantly now slid down her face.

''I know, sweetheart.'' She'd hoped to make them a family, with Rosa. He knew. ''I promise I'll help you get children, but I can't take Mary's baby away from her.''

More than anything, he wanted to reach out to Caroline, take her in his arms and comfort her. But he feared she'd lose control if he moved. He stood stock-still, letting his words touch her with the depth of his feeling.

''Caroline, I'll understand if you don't want to marry me anymore.''

Saying nothing, she put her head down and stepped back.

Mike had dealt with his share of tough-guy criminals in his career, but none of them scared him like this woman in front of him. He held his breath and awaited her answer.

''Do you think that's how I love you, Mike? Only if I get my own way?''

''Caro, I just want you to be happy.''

"I know. So you must believe this Mary deserves to have her baby."

"Yes, I do."

Caroline nodded, still not giving him a clue what she'd say about their future. The tears still fell, though silently now, making tracks on her cheeks, but her breathing had evened.

"Well, Mike," she said finally, "then you'd better tell me what I can do to help her."

Mike couldn't believe his ears. He needed clarification. "Caroline, does that mean you still want to marry me?"

"Of course," Caroline said with a big smile. "If you'll still have me."

Mike couldn't speak, couldn't think. He could only kiss her.

CASEY UNWRAPPED the big book. When he saw it was the picture book of Michael Jordan's career, he let out a whoop. Caroline told him to open it, and he saw the autograph. "Is this real?"

"Yes. Mike asked him for it."

"In person? You actually spoke to Michael Jordan?" Casey demanded in awe.

"Yeah. Sometimes I did security at the Bulls games. He was nice about signing things."

"Oh, man! Wait till I show the guys!" The teenager began to slowly turn the pages, all the laughter and conversation going on around him completely ignored.

Pete leaned over his shoulder, and Casey showed his dad his gift.

Mike watched the family celebrating Christmas. He

had bought a couple of other things for Caroline, and hostess gifts for the Randalls. He'd even found several packages for himself under the tree.

He opened a new cowboy hat—one of the most expensive brands—from Jake and B.J. He decided at once he'd save it to wear on Sundays. Then there was a leather vest from "Santa."

"I didn't know Santa had such good taste," he whispered to Caroline.

"Oh, yes, Santa has the best taste of all."

He opened a smaller package and found a beautiful knife engraved with his name. He looked at Caroline. "This is great!"

"I'm glad you like it," she said with a big smile.

When all the presents had been opened, Caroline asked for a minute of everyone's time. "Mike had to go to town last night because the mother of baby Rosa came back. She's young and scared. The man she was with beat her up. She hitchhiked from Salt Lake City to Rawhide. She loves her baby very much.

"I want to ask if you can help her in any way— with old clothes, a job, a place to live. She needs everything." She looked at her father and her uncle. "I know you always give a gift to the town each Christmas, and I think helping her would be a great gift."

"Where is she now?" her uncle Chad asked.

Mike spoke up. "I lent her my apartment last night, since I was coming back out here. Her mother is dead and her father told her not to come back if she went off with the father of her baby. She's afraid to go home, but she has nowhere else to go." Mike sighed.

"She's made some poor choices, but she loves her baby."

"Of course we'll help," Jake said.

Suddenly all the family was making offers of gifts and donations. But Caroline's aunt Anna had the best offer of all. "I know someone who would welcome Mary and her baby. Mrs. Alexander wants to remain at home, but she needs someone to do light housework and cooking."

"That would be great, Anna," Mike said with a pleased smile. "You Randalls have the biggest hearts in the whole state of Wyoming. I'm pleased to become a member of the family."

"And we're pleased to have you," Jake assured him. "How long before the wedding?"

"As soon as possible," Mike said. "As long as it's okay with Caroline."

She leaned against him. "I think we should join Bill and Margie in their New Year's Eve wedding."

A large cheer went up, led by Bill Metzger.

"Can you get ready that soon?" Mike asked Caroline.

"Of course. We Randalls are experts at planning weddings."

When they were given a few minutes alone, Mike asked for one promise. "I want you to let Jon check you out and make sure you're all right. Okay?"

"All right."

When they took Jon aside to ask him, he promptly agreed. "If you hadn't told me you can't have children, I'd ask if you could be pregnant. Tori says you remind her of herself when she had our first child."

Caroline stared at her partner. Then she stared at Mike.

"Well, Doctor? What do you think?" Mike asked, smiling.

"It couldn't be...could it?"

"Let's go to the office and find out," Mike suggested.

By the time they started to the clinic, half the family knew what was going on. Jake and B.J. followed them in their vehicle.

The other adults started gathering items for the baby's mother, promising to bring things in later. Anna, with Brett, went to town to meet the young woman.

The Randall family was once again playing Santa Claus.

IT DIDN'T TAKE LONG to determine that Caroline was indeed pregnant. She started crying and Mike rocked her against him.

"Don't cry, sweetheart. It's just another special Christmas present from Santa."

She laughed through her tears. "I never thought— I'm so blessed. And you! Don't you get a big head because you managed to get me pregnant."

"Hey, I'm going to brag about it all over town." Then he laughed. "Good thing we're planning a quick wedding. Otherwise, I might be thrown out of town."

She hugged him tightly. "I wouldn't let them do that. Oh, Mike, I'm so happy!"

"Your parents are waiting. Want to go tell them?"

"Oh, yes." She grabbed Mike's arm and Jon's,

too, and the three of them went to the waiting room. Her parents didn't have to ask the question. The answer was all over Caroline's face.

When they stopped hugging her, B.J. told them they'd already made plans for the wedding to be held in the arena at the ranch. Mike looked surprised, but Caroline assured him it would be lovely. Toby and Elizabeth had been married there.

Mike put his arms around her again. "Honey, I'll take you any way I can get you. You're my life. And our baby makes everything perfect."

"I'll remind you of that when the two-o'clock feeding comes around," she told him, delight in her eyes.

"That's a deal," he agreed.

*   *   *   *   *

Judy Christenberry launches a new series for Harlequin American Romance, and you can catch the first story in January in a special anthology from Harlequin Books. Don't miss PRIVATE SCANDALS, available wherever Harlequin Books are sold.

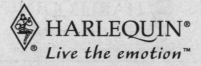

**From Silhouette Books comes
an exciting NEW spin-off to *The Coltons*!**

PROTECTING
PEGGY

by award-winning author
Maggie Price

When FBI forensic scientist
Rory Sinclair checks into
Peggy Honeywell's inn late
one night, the sexy bachelor
finds himself smitten with the
single mother. While Rory works
undercover to solve the mystery
at a nearby children's ranch, his
feelings for Peggy grow...but
will his deception shake the
fragile foundation of their
newfound love?

Coming in December 2003.

THE COLTONS
FAMILY. PRIVILEGE. POWER.

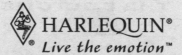

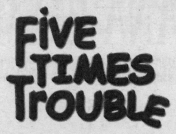
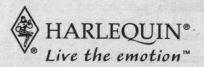

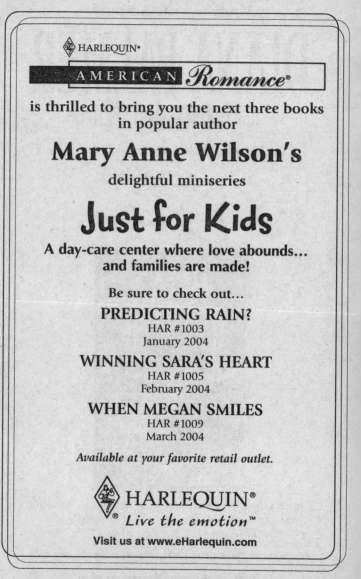